T0113210

Crane Spreads Wings

Also by Susan Trott

The Holy Man's Journey
Tainted Million
The Holy Man
Divorcing Daddy
The Exception
Pursued by the Crooked Man
Sightings
Don't Tell Laura
Incognito
When Your Lover Leaves . . .
The Housewife and the Assassin

For Children

Mr. Privacy
The Sea Serpent of Horse

CRANE SPREADS WINGS

A Bigamist's Story

DOUBLEDAY
New York London Toronto Sydney Auckland

Published by Doubleday
a division of Bantam Doubleday Dell Publishing Group, Inc.
1540 Broadway, New York, New York 10036

Doubleday and the portrayal of an anchor with a dolphin are
trademarks of Doubleday, a division of Bantam Doubleday Dell
Publishing Group, Inc.

Book design by Leah S. Carlson

All of the characters in this book are fictitious, and any resemblance to actual persons, living or dead, is purely coincidental, except for the names of artists and birders.

Library of Congress Cataloging-in-Publication Data
Trott, Susan.
Crane spreads wings: a bigamist's story / Susan Trott
p. cm.
I. Title.
PS3570.R594C7 1998
813'.54—dc21 98-10564
CIP

ISBN 978-0-385-50691-5

Printed in the United States of America

146502721

To Roy, my beloved (and only) husband

To my beloved children: Ann, Emery, and Natalie

To Judyth Weaver, my T'ai Chi teacher,
who I know will forgive any irreverence

To John and Nancy Trott
of the Lanesville Shore House

To Gurdon Saltonstall Worcester,
who first inspired me to be a writer
and who lived at The Quarry

ACKNOWLEDGMENTS

Thanks to the great sculptor Walker Hancock,
who, at age ninety-six, kindly granted me an interview.

Thanks to the great agent Jonathan Dolger.

CONTENTS

Crane Spreads Wings

{1} Crane Spreads Wings

I slipped out of the bridal bed around 6 A.M., if one can still call it a bridal bed after a full month of marriage, if one can call it such on the very day one intends to abandon the groom. Departure bed would be more apt.

Six was my usual awakening time, more like eight for Alan, who, as if dropped from the ceiling, lay sprawled facedown on the departure bed, blissfully unaware that the bed had changed names in the night.

Quickly and quietly, I dressed in jeans, T-shirt, and sweater, then threw a few clothes in a duffel bag on top of my laptop computer and certain books I'd stowed away in the night. I left a pithy farewell note on my bedside table, along with both rings. Although I knew Miss Manners would have let me keep the engagement ring, it had belonged to Alan's grandmother and I thought it should stay in his family. I would only end up pawning it.

I did not take a last look at Alan. Because he had betrayed me, he had become unlovely to me. So I left the room wearing metaphorical blinders but soon doffed them as I descended to the first floor, exited the door to the porch, and jogged down to the sward of green that merged with the coastal rocks.

It was foggy and the tide was rising. The incoming waters did not insist themselves upon the granite boundary but slipped and slapped and swooshed into the crevices and crannies, the tide insinuating itself to its new level without its usual fanfare of crashing waves and airborne spray.

There was no horizon. Ocean and sky were one. The fog seemed to muffle hearing as well as hinder sight, swathing the senses. A blur of yellow revealed itself to be a lone rain-slickered lobsterman in a dory, pulling up pots. On the Big Rock Alan liked to swim to at high tide, three gulls huddled, facing south, and a cormorant stood with outstretched wings, as if posing for a spooky escutcheon.

I loved this summer house, this summer place. I was desolated to leave it, knowing such a lifestyle would probably never come my way again. Still, it was a matter of honor. Alan had misrepresented himself to me. Such behavior could not be brooked.

Slowly, slowly, I began T'ai Chi. I relaxed my body, stilled my mind, let the energy come from the earth through the soles of my feet into my self. I tried to move like the ocean water, like the fog—muffled movements. I smiled when I got to the part of the form called Crane Spreads Wings, looking to the cormorant for approval, although with my right hand above my head and the left held out by my side, it was more of a wings-in-flight pose than the hanging-wings-out-to-dry stance of the cormorant.

Fifteen minutes later I was walking down the rocky road to the main route around Cape Ann. Away from the shore it was warmer. I took off my sweater and stuffed it in my bag. Once on hardtop, I hastened to the village for breakfast at the coffee shop. How I love a coffee shop. It's good for what ails you. Give me six or eight stools along a fresh-wiped counter, a few tables and chairs, the smell of coffee and grease, and a no-nonsense waitress, which was the kind I always tried to be during my years of plying the trade, friendly but seen-it-all, spunky but world-weary. I stoked up on eggs, toast and jam, lots of coffee, and announced to the shop at large that I needed a ride to Rockport if anyone was going that way.

"Train," I said minimally, able to talk as New England as anyone, being a hard-core inhabitant from birth.

An old lady, just leaving, gestured to me and I leapt to follow. We got into a green chevy, which she drove dashingly, one hand on the wheel, the other arm propped on the window-sill, head actually leaning on the headrest, which I'd never seen anyone do.

On the way out of Lanesville we passed the Manship quarry. The sculptor Paul Manship had sort of crept into my Ph.D. thesis in art history, although the thesis was on the relatively unrecognized sculptor Beniamino Bufano. Part of the fight I had with Alan last night was his accusation of my wandering wildly in my thesis. I maintained my wandering wasn't wild, wasn't even wandering; I was only meandering a little, enhancing it thereby.

Paul Manship had a studio here in Lanesville, on one of the marvelous granite quarries that, once emptied of rocks in the last century to pave streets and build buildings, had filled with spring water and become huge rock-hewn private lakes. Here Manship had conceived the fabulous *Prometheus Bringing Fire* fountain for Rockefeller Center in 1934.

What Alan and I were doing here in Lanesville at his mother's summer house was writing: my thesis, Alan's novel. It took me the whole month to realize he wasn't writing, that the much-vaunted novel I'd heard about all through our courting days, supposedly in its final draft, didn't exist at all. It was hot air. He was hot air. After he wrongly accused me of not sticking to the point in my thesis, I hit him with my pent-up disappointment regarding his phantom novel.

I had come to the realization he was hot air before I discovered the spectral aspect of his novel. I'd begun to suspect knavery early on, so I was superalert to his behavior in general. One day he was regaling a group of admirers and I thought to myself, there he goes, spouting off again, and was horrified that I viewed my groom as a spouter. How could I love or feel sexy about, or in any way admire, a spouter or one whose lips I conceived as billowing forth hot air. At Harvard, where we had met, he was a brilliant teacher of Shakespeare and had won my heart forsooth and forthwith, but it was his being a creative person, a novelist, that had won my hand. I am not a creative person myself, but they seem to me the only ones worth being with for any length of time. Many uncreative people are worth knowing too, but those ones who are not worth the time of day at all, let alone years of marriage, are people with pretensions to creativity, spouters, even if they really know their Shakespeare and are killingly attractive from the front.

It was shortly after the spouting realization that I saw Alan from the back one day while standing on the lawn and it occurred to me he didn't have any neck to speak of. His shoulders appeared to grow out of his earlobes. There was no space between his hairline and his collar line. From the front he had a neck along with the requisite Adam's apple verifying his manhood, but from the back he was a no-neck and could I, an art historian, admire, love, or feel sexy about one who, even passing fair from the front, would always let me down aesthetically from the back?

If he had truly written his novel, if he didn't ever spout, then the no-neck wouldn't have mattered at all—but there it was, I had to leave him, even though it meant giving up the diamond ring and seaside home and, well, yes, love.

The two sculptors, Benny Bufano and Paul Manship, had met each other in New York City. Benny was a poor Italian immigrant living in a small apartment with his mother, his father, and fifteen brothers and sisters. Although a teenager, he was already a dedicated artist. Manship at that time had been given a commission for the Panama Pacific International Exposition. He hired Benny to assist in completing the enlargements for the models in San Francisco. It was Benny's first big job and he went on his way rejoicing. I now decided that I too would go to San Francisco, where I would be able to see all of Benny's work.

Surely my being so deeply subsumed in the lives of these creative hardworking sculptors served to make Alan's hot-airness particularly unspeakable and my betrayed-bride status unendurable. But Alan did misrepresent himself to me. He was false. I had believed in him. Whenever he spoke of the novel, I encouraged him with all my heart because it seemed such a good story and in the telling he would combine intellect and art. It is hard for a teacher of Shakespeare to set pen to paper because one is so humbled by the Bard's untouchable greatness. I respected Alan for being able to make that leap, but it turns out he didn't make that leap, not even a little stumbling step.

But I was not going to think any more about him.

My ride and I were almost to Rockport. Being New Englanders, we didn't have to converse, once we'd commented brusquely on the fog, which was now lifting, and on the driver ahead of us, who couldn't settle on a steady speed but went now fast, now slow.

"Man in a hat," said my ride.

"Right," said I, for it is a given that a man in a hat in a sedan will be a terrible driver. A man in a hat in a truck will not be so bad.

I thanked the woman and got out of the car. I stood by the tracks for the first leg of my journey to the other coast, the coast where people lived, talked, and laughed flamboyantly.

Luckily, I had savings. I have always been a saver. I've always worked and always saved. When I was five and my mother gave me a quarter for the week's help around the apartment, I saved a dime of it. When I was old enough to get part-time jobs, I gave Mom half and saved half of the other half. First it was a piggy bank, then a savings bank. Now it was mutual funds. University, even as a scholarship student, even doing waitressing on the side, depleted my savings, but I had enough left to get to San Francisco and live in a cheap hotel while I looked for work and a place to live.

Benny Bufano made two dollars a day on the Manship sculptures and lived in Chinatown, probably delighted to be with other short people because Benny, like me, was only five feet tall. Later he went to China itself, to Szechwan, where the famous pottery was made. He lived there three years, learning the method, living like a Chinese laborer, working for his daily bowl of rice. Benny lived life fearlessly, to the hilt. I would too. I was twenty-three and my life was all before me. Even if I couldn't create a novel or piece of music or work of art, I could create my life.

Crane spreads wings!

The train rocketed into the station and I climbed aboard, throwing my duffel up to the rack above me, sitting down, leaning back with my legs on the opposite seat. Superimposed on the passing greenery was my head of glossy brown hair, large green eyes, thin face, and lips curved in a smile. I felt so happy, it almost made me wonder if I'd falsified some of Alan's falseness, just to get away.

"Mrs. Crackalbee? Emma? I'm sorry to call you so early, but is Jane there?"

"Alan, are you all right? Are you crying?"

"It's just allergies."

"I don't expect her, Alan. Why would she leave the shore today? It's going to be ninety here!"

"Please have her call me right away if she shows up. It's terribly important."

"Of course I will, but as I say . . ."

"Thank you. As soon as she gets there."

"You might try . . ."

"I have. I've tried everyone. But I'm sure she'll go to you. Goodbye."

"Wait! You can't just call and worry me about my daughter, then say goodbye. What's going on?"

"She's left me. I woke up and found the rings on her bedside table."

"If you have been unkind to my Effie . . ."

"I swear that I haven't. Talk to her. Please tell her to come back. I love her."

{2} Crane Droops Wings

I got to Mom's apartment at ten o'clock, the same two-bedroom apartment on Commonwealth Avenue in Boston she'd lived in since she married my dad at twenty. Everything was still the same for Mom. For twenty-five years she'd worked in the same law firm as a secretary and for two weeks every summer she rented the same tiny cottage on the same little lake in New Hampshire. She'd never been anywhere else in the world until the year I took her to the Vietnam Veterans Memorial in D.C. to find my father's name on the shimmering stone, the father my two sisters had never known, being infants when he went to war, and whom I remembered only dimly.

My sisters still lived with Mom. They were going to be secretaries too and were in secretarial school, although it's hard to believe such schools still exist with typing and shorthand virtually defunct. I suppose they learn computer skills and how to tell the boss to make his own fucking coffee. I never was and never would be a secretary, despite the fact that Mom—perversely, it seemed to me, possibly cripplingly—named me after a famous secretary, the one in *The Maltese Falcon:* Effie, a dreadful name. What was it even short for? At thirteen, I'd appropriated my austere middle name: Jane. Maybe, since I was going to San Francisco, I would reclaim Effie, which suddenly struck me as playful and feisty, calmly pugnacious, the name of a T'ai Chi warrior re-creating her life.

But Mom was proud of her profession, proud she'd supported and raised her three girls, particularly proud that I'd gone to Harvard, although she couldn't understand why, with my brains, if I was going for an advanced degree, I didn't become a lawyer. Lawyers were gods to her. And lawyers made astronomical sums. Art historians didn't. Sometimes they didn't even find jobs. We had endless talks about it. It broke her heart. She pleaded with me. She didn't understand. It was hopeless.

Then I redeemed myself by marrying Alan Croy, an assistant professor at Harvard from a fine old Boston family. To my mom, it was a miracle. How her eyes lit up with wonder when she first came to the Croys' summer house. She would sit on the porch by the hour, looking at the ocean, awed, as if she'd never seen the ocean before, which maybe she hadn't, beyond the occasional glimpse of Boston Harbor. A far cry from the small New Hampshire bebloodsuckered lake, this spangled, endless, sinuous sea.

"Effie, honey." She greeted me with a hug and kiss. "Alan called. He wants you to call him right away. But first, sit down, sweetie. I'll pour you a coffee. We've got to talk about this."

Which meant I had to listen. That was okay. That was the price I had to pay, the Rubicon I had to cross. She would make me feel like a kid again, a stupid kid who didn't know what life was all about. And she was right. It was she who had the experience of life, of a hard, thankless, work-filled, shabby life, prey to her lawyer gods, who paid her a crummy salary and had affairs with her and allowed her a crummy two weeks off a year. She was the one who should have been a lawyer, gone to night school, but how, with three little kids and no husband and only the occasional lawyer lover who would never in a million years marry her, only give her an hour here, an hour there, every callous fuck injecting the hope that he would be the one to change her life.

Now she was forty-five and fat and her hair was dyed, her makeup ill-applied—but she was a wonderful woman and I admired her more than anyone on earth. She was not hot air.

I sat down on the couch and rested my head on its back where an afghan covered the wear and tear. It's old wool smell was a comfort. It had been around forever, originally crocheted by God knows who. The room was furnished in American Stuffed and it was doodad heaven. Every table held china animals, little boxes, pictures in tawdry frames, and even, God forgive her, plastic bouquets. The pictures on the wall weren't paint-by-number but were of their ilk, one step above. Still, the room was clean and cheerful and cozy. It was a real room and it was home.

I suddenly wanted to go down the little hall to my old bedroom and crawl under the covers. It would be so much easier than going three thousand miles across the entire North American continent to a city where I didn't know a soul to start a new life. I felt the bedroom calling me. *Effie! Effie!* The idea was compelling. I could have a small nervous breakdown, something I've always felt I owed myself. Mom would bring me food and worry about me and take precious sick days off to be by my side. She was a mother who always gave her all. It made me wonder if, under the guise of going to San Francisco to study Bufano, I wasn't simply, classically, running home to mother. If so, wouldn't that constitute my being full of hot air, even though spouting off only to myself?

She put the cups and saucers on the coffee table and sat down next to me. "Did he hit you?"

"No."

Mom always told us if a man raised a hand to us, walk right out of the door and don't look back.

"Is he a drunkard?"

"No. And he wasn't unfaithful to me either. There's no other woman."

She always said you don't necessarily walk out the door if there's another woman (having been one so many times herself and learned it didn't mean anything). Drunkenness was fairly okay too. No man is perfect. But these were the only three possible crimes. Being a spouter and a misrepresenter would not enter her lawyerly mind as possible marital felonies. And no-neckism wasn't even in the picture.

This was going to be a tough talk. A Scotch whiskey would do wonders to help get me through it, speaking of drunkenness.

"I married too soon, Mom. I haven't really lived yet. I don't love Alan. I thought I did, but I don't. He's not the man I thought he was."

"It's these artists." She came at me from left field.

"What?"

"These artists of yours. All your life you're thinking and reading and writing about these artists. Always in another world. I'll bet you had it in your mind Alan was an artist and now you've found out he's not and so he's not good enough for you. Smart, handsome, a professor, money, good family—that's not enough, right? He should also paint pictures, make clay figurines with glazes . . ." (which I'd told her about Benny doing in Szechwan). "Effie, you're breaking my heart."

She did look stricken. I almost felt afraid for her. I figured I'd better cut this short. I stood up and seized my bag, holding it as if it were an Uzi I was leveling at her as I backed toward the door. "I'm going to San Francisco, Mom, leaving today."

"Don't do this, Effie. You'll regret it all your life. You'll end up like me."

Her words were tragic. I felt like crying so got mad instead. "It's my life, damn it. Respect it. Respect my work. Respect me."

"Don't go, Effie" were the last broken-hearted words I heard as I slammed out the door.

Benny Bufano's grandmother had left her life savings of two thousand dollars to the sixteen Bufano children. Benny was going to give his share to his mother, but then things turned bad for him. He wasn't getting commissions in New York and his girlfriend was pregnant. He wanted to go back to San Francisco, where he felt he had a chance at becoming great—and where he could keep the pregnancy a secret. He asked his mother if he could borrow the entire two thousand and pay it back when he was famous. She was shocked. She took one hundred and twenty-five dollars from the glass jar and said, "This is your share, Benny. This is all you get." He took his share then, right in front of her, he stole the rest. From his old work-worn, beaten-down mother, he took the jar full of money and ran out the door.

My parting glimpse of Mom must have been similar to his of his mother, a love-shattered face, aged ten years. But I hadn't stolen mere money. I'd stolen the hopes and dreams she had for me.

"Hello?"

"Alan, what's wrong? You sound utterly despairing."

"Who is this?"

"It's your mother, for God's sake! I should think you'd know my voice after twenty-eight years of vocals—from lullabies to drunken rages!"

"Jane has left me."

"That bitch! I never trusted her. Did she take the rings?"

"No, she did not. And I refuse to listen to you malign her."

"I've held my tongue all this time. Please let me malign her just a little. It's such an opportune time. And it will do you good."

"I'm going to do everything I can to get her back. I'm hoping she'll have a change of heart and walk in the door any minute. So why say something you'll regret?"

"You should thank your lucky stars. There was something distinctly funny about her. For one thing, she had the most obsessive distrust of lawyers."

"Who doesn't?"

"It always made me suspect she had something to hide."

"Well, she doesn't."

"And that mother! You would have been saddled with her all your life. You know Jane would want to take her in when she got old."

"You mean in thirty years?"

"See! You already sound much better. I am sorry, darling. I know you loved her. She was smart and a good dresser and I have to hand it to her, for a small woman she never let herself be adorable."

"Please don't talk about her in the past tense."

"Come to think of it, why did she leave you?"

"I don't know."

"I'm sure it was because her criminal past was catching up with her. She had to get out of town."

"I don't need to listen to this shit."

"It was quite fine of her, really, to leave the diamonds—which are legally hers."

"Goodbye, Mother. I'll talk to you later."

"A tout à l'heure."

"I don't speak French. Goodbye."

"Au revoir, darling. You did once. It's never too late to relearn it. And now you'll have time on your hands. God forbid you'd use it to write your novel."

———

I stood outside my mom's building suffering a supreme loss of confidence. No longer the T'ai Chi warrior. Crane droops wings! The fact was: Aside from brief vagabonding trips, museuming around Europe, I'd never really left home (i.e., the Boston area) for any length of time. I was devoted to Mom and even to my idiotic sisters. The truth was: I was devoted to Alan too. He'd been my best friend for the last two years. So I felt alone and lost. Also, I badly needed to pee. I had intended to do so at Mom's, but my hasty departure frustrated the intention.

Just then my two sisters showed up, Ellie and Edna—yes, sad to say, all our names begin with E. "Effie, have you come to visit?" They rushed into my arms for hugs and kisses, even kissing each other. They were very affectionate, like puppies. They had a couple of inches on me, but we would always be the little Crackalbee girls. Mom was a normal size. I don't know where the runtism came from. If Dad was so short, how did he get in the Army? Ellie and Edna were three and four years younger than me and sometimes I wondered if they had the same dad as me—they were so stupid.

Ellie had blonde curls and Edna was a redhead. They had gorgeous hair but plain faces. I had the noticeable face but ordinary hair, straight and brown. We were all slim and strong.

"Didn't I tell you it was Effie?" said Edna. "Ellie didn't believe me when I said that was you in front of the building," she explained needlessly.

"I did too believe you," Ellie complained, "but she had a bag. Why would she have a bag if she was Effie?"

They bickered about it. It was the typical type of subject their dim wits liked to seize upon—whether having a bag meant I was Effie or not.

"Well, you can see it is Effie and she does have a bag," said Edna. "Why do you?" Edna asked.

"Have a bag," Ellie clarified as I knew she would, but I'd long ago gotten past the urge to throttle either one of them, having decided that they were endearing. They haven't a mean bone in their bodies, whereas I have many mean bones.

"I thought I was going to San Francisco, but now I'm not so sure. Will you please tell Mom that maybe I'm not going to San Francisco? I'll call her with my decision. And tell her not to tell Alan."

"Not to tell Alan that you're not going to San Francisco?" Edna asked.

Stymied, I pondered the question. In my sisters' company, it was amazing how quickly I sank to their intellectual level. It was like a quick-acting virus. I didn't have any idea what Mom should not tell Alan.

"If you're not going to San Francisco," asked Ellie, "what about the bag, then?"

"Right," I said. Always a good response with them, it seemed to satisfy.

"I've got to go. I have to pee like mad."

"But, Effie, you can't go to a public rest room. You know how you are. Come back inside."

"No. I can't do that. We've just had a scene. Goodbye," I said in a flurry of more hugs and kisses.

"Call us!" they pleaded.

"Yes, I'll talk to you soon. I'll call." They always needed assurance that I'd be in touch. I think I needed it too.

I have a morbid fear of public rest rooms. It's not about inherent disease. It's about getting locked in. Trapped. Gas station rest rooms are the worst. They never have any windows—maybe one inaccessible one over the door, usually covered for some reason with wire grating. Restaurant rest rooms don't have windows either and if trapped I don't feel I can shout, "Help, let me out!" because they seem soundproofed, maybe because they are often near the kitchen, where the ongoing racket would drown out my panicky cries.

Across Commonwealth Avenue the VERITAS flag billowed and waved, signifying The Harvard Club. Alan was a member. I could use the divine bathroom there and also the phone to arrange for a flight in the event my wings started to spread again. I could even have lunch were it not for the blue jeans, but these could be changed in the yearned-for ladies' room. Then, once suitably attired, I'd order a Scotch on the rocks with a twist of lemon to make it look less grim, to give it a little saffron glow, before downing it in one gulp.

{3} Crane Looks Around

"Hello?"

"Alan, this is Emma Crackalbee."

"Thank God! Have you seen Jane?"

"Yes, she came by. She's not going to San Francisco."

"Was she?"

"She seemed to think she was, but now I hear from the girls that she's not, or at least she's undecided."

"But where is she now?"

"The girls just saw her outside the building. Alan, she seems very confused to me."

"I don't understand any of this. I woke up and saw the rings on the bedside table and she wasn't in the house. She always goes right to work on her thesis after breakfast."

"Was there a note?"

"Well . . ."

"What did the note say, Alan?"

"You talked to her. What did she tell you?"

"She said you didn't hit her or drink or have another woman."

"What did I do, then?"

"What does the note say? I'm her mother, I have a right to know. I know it's personal and hard for you to tell, but I'm afraid I must insist. I'm worried about her. Has she been drinking?"

"Not much. Constitutionally, she can't drink much because she's so little that she's flying after one drink. She wishes she could drink more. She tries to build up her tolerance, but by the end of the second drink, she falls asleep."

"Is it something about your sex life?"

"No, Emma, it's . . . it's so stupid. She says I misrepresented myself. She says she married me with the understanding that I was writing a novel and now she thinks she's discovered that I'm not writing a novel."

"For Effie this is very serious, Alan."

"It's just that we have different working methods. It could be she's troubled about her own work, which tends to wander. In any event, I thought we married for love. To be together! 'To have and to hold from this day forth!' "

"I have a feeling she might show up and give you another chance."

"Do you think so? I hope so. I'll do anything. I love her, Emma."

"I believe you. Goodbye, Alan."

I mounted the stone steps of The Harvard Club and entered the gracious lounge area. Outsized red leather furniture stood mostly empty. It was deliciously cool. In the ladies' room, I relieved myself of the Lanesville and Crackalbee coffee buildup, then washed and put on a skirt and sandals and silk tee, mashing the jeans and cotton T-shirt into the duffel bag.

A tormented-looking heavyset man was using the phone,

so I sat down in the big armchair to wait and to use the reprieve to ponder. Mom's horror at my leaving Alan had taken the courage from me. I began to think she was right. I had been hasty. I hadn't given the marriage a chance. Maybe he was so excited at being on his honeymoon, he simply hadn't gotten into the writing groove. I had judged and condemned too quickly. As for the spouting and the shoulders being so near the ear line, well, those could be dealt with over time. I'd think of something.

A little boy came out of the men's room and sat down near me, looking even more lost in the enormous chair than I did. He had a mass of dark curls, sparkling brown eyes, and was short and chunky. We greeted each other and he began telling me in admirable detail about a movie he'd seen, one that struck me as outstandingly inappropriate for his seven or eight years. It even had Sylvester Stallone in it. I was enthralled.

Then the tormented hunched-over man came from the phone. Seeing me, his features untwisted themselves and he even looked less heavy, standing tall with relief. He smiled, showing unnerving, sort of scary-looking teeth in an otherwise kindly face. "You're here!" he exclaimed joyfully.

He meant me. It's true I was here. Still . . .

He put out his hand. "I'm Gled Saltonstall. I see you've met Danny."

Danny, in the midst of a particularly florid scene, during which he actually used the word *penis,* continued to describe the movie, raising his voice over Gled, whom I presumed to be his father. Same dark curls, although not in such a mass, clipped short and organized with a side part. I wondered if Gled, like Effie, was not short for any sort of real name but was a name entire to itself and felt sorry for him, despite his fabulous tigerish teeth. My teeth were slightly bucked on top and the bottoms were jumbled. Mom couldn't afford orthodonture, so I was very tooth-conscious.

"Danny, be quiet," he told his son firmly. Danny subsided good-naturedly.

"Effie Crackalbee," I introduced myself.

"But . . . that's not the right name."

"I'm not surprised."

"Aren't you going to take care of me, then?" Danny asked.

"You see, we're off to our summer place for vacation and we were to have met the *au pair* here an hour ago. Danny's mother hired her. And she hasn't shown up. And Danny's mother has left for Paris. I'm at my wit's end."

"Couldn't you be my *pair?*" Danny asked hopefully, having found the listener of his dreams.

"Danny, son, obviously Ms. Crackalbee isn't sitting here in The Harvard Club hoping for a nanny job."

"To tell you the truth, I'm rather at my wit's end also. I accept the position. As long as you're not a lawyer."

"I'm a pilot."

I was surprised. He seemed pudgy for a pilot and his face seemed too gentle. But the teeth were definitely pilotish and his brown eyes had the clear, unfettered, slightly mystical gaze one thinks of pilots having, if one ever thinks of pilots. I haven't until now or perhaps I have, since I have these preconceived ideas—probably combining Saint-Exupéry and Tom Cruise.

"That's right. He is a pilot," Danny said a little hectically, wanting so much for me to be his *pair.* "He's a really great pilot."

"That's fine." I smiled reassuringly. "Please tell me the terms of employment."

Gled responded eagerly. "You'll have your own room and board and a thousand dollars a month with two days off a week and most nights, except for when you are especially requested to remain. I'll be coming up to town periodically, but the idea is that I get to spend time with Danny. I'm divorced from his mother. There is also a couple who lives at the house for cleaning and gardening who are great pals of Danny's, so your duties will not be strenuous."

I looked dubious. "There is a great deal of responsibility involved. I think I should get two thousand a month at the very least. No wonder the nanny didn't show up."

I thought he would compromise at fifteen hundred, but he colored and said, submissively and un-Tom-Cruise-like, "Two thousand will be fine. I have no idea of the going rates. I just trust my wife in these matters, but she is a tightwad."

"She is not," said Danny loyally.

"But are you to trust me on sight to care for your boy?"

"Yes. I trust my intuition. But tell me about yourself."

"Well, there isn't much to tell. I'm from Boston, across the avenue as a matter of fact. I went to Harvard. I'm an art historian and I'm writing my thesis. I'm twenty-three."

I waited for him to say that I looked seventeen, but to his credit, he didn't. He only said happily, "Very good. Let's go. This is great. I didn't go to Harvard, however. I don't want to give a false impression by being here. My sister did. She's the smart one of the family."

"I'm smart," said Danny.

"Very smart," Gled agreed.

I guess my thinking, if I was thinking at all, was that I only had two thousand dollars saved up, exactly what Benny stole, but it wouldn't go as far for me as it had for him in 1918. It was a fortune then. A month as Danny's nanny would give me another two thousand and also time to reconsider and not go off half-cocked.

I realized that another thing wrong with being married to Alan was that for the first time in my life I wasn't earning and saving. I didn't need to anymore, but it didn't feel right. I felt insecure. It was a comfort to have money of my own and see it build. Possibly I was some sort of miser.

Or maybe I took the job because I was actually having my small nervous breakdown and was no longer accountable for my actions.

I rose from the chair on my mighty T'ai Chi legs, not having to push up with my arms, and bent for my duffel bag, which Gled beat me to, seizing it with a jubilant smile, as though this were the best day of his life, then dropping a shoulder under the weight of the books.

"Anything you want before we go? It's an hour trip."

I decided not to say a Scotch on the rocks, thereby shattering his trust in his intuition. Possibly he had intuited that this was a woman who occasionally slugged down a noonday whiskey, but I doubted it.

Danny put on his baseball cap backward and stood ready to go. He was wearing shorts and a shirt that would better fit his father if his father liked wearing his clothes really loose. "Skateboard?" I asked.

"It's in the car," he said.

Danny and Gled looked at me with total approval and off we went into the heat of the day.

Crane lifts head and looks into distance from both sides. But doesn't lift wings.

{4} Crane Huddles Out of the Wind

I woke up looking at blue sky, sensing rapid movement, feeling baffled, but there wasn't the usual fear that comes with not knowing where the hell you are or what's going on. There was almost a feeling of enjoyment, of being cast utterly adrift and no longer being answerable. Crane huddles out of the wind.

Too soon it came to me that I was a newly hired nanny lying down in the back of a convertible car going somewhere for the summer. I'd left my groom, run home to Mother, run away from Mother, gone to The Harvard Club to drink, and gotten hired as a nanny instead.

Imagine my surprise when I sat up and looked around, only to discover I was returning to the very village I'd left that morning. Lanesville. There was the firehouse. Now we were coming down the hill to Plum Cove Beach and I could see the point of land on which stood the house next to Alan's.

Now we were coming up the hill from the beach and the Little League field. There was the white wooden Catholic Church, Sacred Heart, across from which was the rocky road I'd taken from Alan's house on my first steps to the—ha ha—West

Coast of America. What if Gled Saltonstall turned onto that road? Maybe he'd been asked to find me at The Harvard Club and return me to Alan under the guise of hiring me as a nanny.

But we did not turn left onto the shore road. We turned right, inland. So it was simply an amazing coincidence that both these men had summer houses in the same tiny village on Cape Ann. However, the chances were good that they didn't know each other. Gled looked older than Alan and summer inland people didn't mix with summer shore people. Year-round village people didn't mix with either. Alan never came inland. He rarely went to the village. He just stayed at the shore and friends came to him or he went to Boston. Sometimes he drove five miles to the sickeningly charming village of Annisquam to sail from the yacht club there or play tennis, especially if it would serve to keep him from writing his novel that day.

Sometimes I went with him and shot pool at the club, not knowing how to play tennis or sail or, for that matter, swim. A city secretary's child doesn't learn luxury sports and there's no old swimming hole on Commonwealth Avenue. Two weeks a year at the slimy lake in New Hampshire didn't do the job, although I have a small memory of dog-paddling around before I shunned the water entirely. There's the YMCA if you're a chlorine junkie, but I was an art junkie. Although I did go to the Y for T'ai Chi, praise be, starting at age sixteen. It brought me calm and balance in a nerve-wracking world. I no longer bite my nails or jiggle my leg. I don't fall down, except on icy winter sidewalks, and no one can push me down either. I sleep at night. I don't get sick or, so far, old. No more headaches. My feet point straight ahead when I walk. Head up. My shoulders are relaxed. My arms hang down and swing loosely, softly. My hands are soft, my elbows, all my joints are soft and easy. Not a clench to be found, except maybe sometimes, like today, in my jaw. I have orgasms too. What a woman, eh? Except what am I doing in this car that turned right instead of left? What a simple solution it would have been after all if Gled were taking me home to Alan, delivering me up to my rightful groom.

We drove a mile and a half down an ever-narrowing road into the woods. I knew this road. Walker Hancock, another great sculptor, lived on a quarry at the end of it, still lived there, ninety years old. It had seemed so amazing to me to discover that two great sculptors lived on quarries here in Lanesville that I'd briefly got waylaid in my thesis writing, looking into Hancock's work, which celebrated the nobility of the human spirit. He'd been awarded the National Medal of Arts for "His extraordinary contribution to the art of sculpture and for demonstrating the enduring beauty of the classical tradition." His quarry had always been open for Lanesville kids to swim in, speaking of swimming holes. The quarries, once the rock was excavated from them, filled up with soft, fresh, spring water and apparently supplied the most wonderful silken swimming in the world, keeping a constant seventy-two degrees all summer.

Now, passing by Hancock's, we entered a private driveway, swept around a curve, and a quarry was revealed to my eyes, about the size of a football field with a long, low, shingled house at the far end, green grass and flowers all about, and a tennis court on the bluff above. Slender birches made a woodland of dalmatian trunks and fluttering leaves. It was a hidden wonderland.

Father and son were grinning. Gled eased the car to a stop before stone steps leading up to the lawn. It was only seconds before they were out of the car, out of their clothes, and into the quarry.

Mary and George Flanagan divested the car of its luggage and showed me to my room, which was over the garage, in the trees, out of the wind.

Dear Janice:

I hope you are not minding these daily letters, which in any case you don't have to answer because, inspired by the wonderful ease of e-mail, I am using you for a sounding board, or a journal, you being the only one I can go on and on about Effie to. Effie has been with us four days now and Danny is as smitten as I am. She will watch him skateboard by the hour, cheering his every hard-won new move. Unfortunately, she can't swim, so Danny can only swim in the quarry when I am here. However, she takes him to Plum Cove Beach, where there are plenty of people and the water isn't over his head like the "bottomless" quarry, the thought of which unsettles her.

She begins and ends every day with her T'ai Chi, standing on the high bluff above the quarry where you and I like to dive from. I am entranced by the slow relaxed movements, the poised postures. Maybe one day, when I have declared my undying devotion, she can teach it to me and I can teach her to swim and play tennis. I have begun teaching her to drive the quarry hackabout, so she can take Danny to the beach and village. Imagine someone so deprived of these basic skills, yet so far advanced in her education! I am surprised at you, checking up that she really went to Harvard, but I'm glad all is on the up-and-up.

It's wonderful to be with Danny so much. He is a treasure. More later.

Love,
Gledbury

Gledman:

Okay, I'm sorry about checking out her Harvardity, but a pickup is a pickup—Harvard Club or no Harvard Club. You picked up this woman and brought her into your home to look after your dearest treasure, knowing nothing about her. And, mind you, Harvard has no longer the cachet it used to have. Anyone goes there, just like any other university.

It sure sounds like you've picked a winner. For an *au pair.* But to love? Twenty-three? Also, T'ai Chi is for pussies.

Love,

Janice

"Hi, Edna. It's Effie."

"Effie, you said you'd call us and it's been six days!"

"Five."

"I'm counting the day we saw you. That was Saturday. So Saturday, Sunday, Monday . . ."

"Okay, six."

"You've never gone so long without calling Mom."

"Edna, I'm twenty-three years old. I should be able to go months without calling home!"

"Are you in San Francisco?"

"No."

"Thank goodness. Ellie! Mom! She's not in San Francisco. Effie, here's Mom."

"Effie. How could you do this to us? We've been worried sick."

"I'm sorry, Mom. I've been huddling."

"And Alan. That poor man is at the end of his rope."

"Probably because his tennis game is off."

"Oh, Effie. Sometimes you do seem hard-hearted. What did he do to you? Nothing. It's only something he didn't do, which really is none of your business, whether he writes a novel or not. It's not as if his income depends upon it. Well, never mind. Where are you?"

"I can't say. But I've got a job and I'll call you regularly from now on and I . . . I guess I'll speak to Alan."

"But why this hiding?"

"I don't know exactly. I just feel like it. It's doing me good."

" 'Huddling,' you called it. Why do you call it 'huddling'?"

"I think of myself as a crane, you see."

"Cranes fly long distances and have amazing far-carrying voices. Isn't it the crane that brings babies? Are you pregnant?"

"No, that's the stork. Same family. Goodbye, Mom. I love you. Don't worry about me. And I promise to speak to Alan and to call you soon again."

"Goodbye, honey."

Although I'd said assuredly the stork was the same family, I didn't know. I didn't know anything about cranes. Mom seemed to know more than I did. Her knowledge constantly surprised me. She had a fabulous memory. Oh, the things Mom might have done if she could have spread her wings!

I wandered into Gled's living room. The wood-paneled walls curved into the ceiling, paneling it as well, giving a warm glow to the whole room. The walls on either side of the fireplace were shelved with books. There was a Steinway grand piano, on which Gled liked to pound out marches, and several groupings of slip-covered couches and chairs in pastel hues on priceless rugs. The most often occupied furniture cluster was by the many-paned bay window that overlooked the quarry. The artwork on the walls was good stuff, including old Japanese woodcut prints. There was a Hiroshige of two cranes. One of the birds is standing in marsh water, bill open, perhaps, as Mom said, making its remarkable call, and the other, partial body, wings spread, is swooping down from the top, as if flying from beyond the frame into the picture, its bill like a Samurai sword descending on the unwary below.

Among the thousand books shelved at either side of the fireplace, I found a 1917 *Birds of America* with color plates by Louis Agassiz Fuertes and read about the Great Blue Heron, also called Blue Crane. It sounded exactly like a T'ai Chi warrior. Alert, farsighted, able to stand motionless for long periods, a stealthy skillful fisher and hunter, it stands with its neck coiled in an S-shape, then lengthens it to strike more quickly than the eye can follow—its bill like a rapier. It can walk in the water without causing a ripple. It is solitary, except when breeding.

This was all very satisfying, but upon closer reading, I found that the Blue Crane was not of the crane family at all but of the Order of Herons, Storks, Ibises, Etc. Whereas cranes are of the Order of Marsh Dwellers and it is the crane that has the famous voice, especially the five-foot-tall Whooping Crane because of its super-long larynx but also the Sandhill Crane. It does fly huge distances at high speed and rises to tremendous heights so that it often can't be seen from below. It is a fine brave bird, full of courage, alertness, and strength, never off-guard. When at bay, it will fight for its life, using its bill to vicious advantage. This is not a huddling bird. I have shamed the name of crane.

About its voice, the book says:

> This cry of the Sandhill Crane is a veritable voice of Nature, untamed and unterrified. Its uncanny quality is like that of the Loon, but is more pronounced because of the much greater volume. Its resonance is remarkable and its carrying power is increased by a distinct tremolo effect. Often for several minutes after the birds have vanished, the unearthly sound drifts back to the listener, like a taunting trumpet from the underworld.

Wow!

I sought out Gled, who was playing a rousing game of checkers with Danny, and asked him if I could borrow the hefty volume.

"Help yourself to anything, Effie. Our home is your home. On second thought, don't take the family silver. My sister, Janice, is attached to it."

I took the book back to my room and put it by my bed. I wanted to know more about birds.

"Hello?"

"Hello, Gled. It's Lynn."

"Lynn?"

"Your ex-wife."

"Calling from Paris? It's not like you. Is anything wrong?"

"Yes, there is something damn wrong. I heard from the *au pair* that she never hooked up with you and you know our agreement was that Danny could only stay with you if there was someone to look after him besides you and the Flanagans."

"I found a wonderful girl. Danny is crazy about her. He's in good hands. Please don't worry. Have a wonderful vacation and don't worry."

"I can't help it. You're such a wild man. Promise me you and Danny won't do anything dangerous."

"I've promised until I'm blue in the face. You've got to trust me."

"Don't let him skateboard where there are cars. Don't let him swim alone in the quarry. Don't let him dive off the cliff. Is your girl a good swimmer?"

"Olympic-caliber. Have fun in France. Goodbye."

{5} Repulse Monkey (Stepping Backward)

There are thirty-seven moves in the Wang Short Form of T'ai Chi. The twentieth is called Repulse Monkey or what my teacher's teacher, Cheng Man-chi'ing called Step Back to Drive the Monkey Away. You walk backward, pointing your feet exactly straight ahead, shifting your weight to the planted foot, rooting it while moving the opposite arm back, then circling it forward in a piercing motion. It is a strange, complicated move. Well, all of the T'ai Chi moves are. They are all moves that one has never moved before.

You can keep on going backward as long as you want until you decide to step out into the Diagonal Flying posture, which is not unlike Crane Spreads Wings, except that the weight is on the front foot instead of the back and the body is on the diagonal and there is more a feeling of flying than of simple wing-spreading—of action rather than imminent action.

The stepping backward, as well as being good for repulsing monkeys or humans, is apparently good for depression, so I was doing a lot of Repulse Monkey in my morning and evening forms, just in case I was depressed.

Since I'd given up the idea of huddling because it shamed the crane, I now thought of myself as stepping back to drive all the monkeys away—the monkeys being Alan and my family. I was stepping back to get the view, to see what was in front of me, stepping back to see where I was going and where I had been.

I knew that, despite my inland quarry sanctuary, it would not be possible to elude Alan the whole summer long. The chances were good that he'd see me somewhere or hear tell of me, so I figured I'd better go see him and get it over with. He was driving Mom crazy with his calls. I still had not told her where I was but had told her the nature of the job. My sisters, puzzled, inquired whether being a nanny was a step up or down from being a waitress. They were unable to understand why I, the brain of the family, continued to take lowly jobs while scorning their secretarial endeavors. When I tried to explain about writing my thesis, they wondered why, if I was going to spend years writing something, I didn't just write a novel that people could buy and read. "Right," I said.

So, having been almost a week at the quarry with Danny and Gled, I set off for Alan's on my first night off. I walked the mile and a half to the road and then the quarter mile to the shore. Along with my other disorders, I didn't drive. Gled, dismayed, was teaching me on the old quarry Toyota, so I could drive Danny to the beach. Meanwhile, Danny and I were happy to walk (and skateboard) the distance. I was a quick learner. I wonder why Alan never taught me to drive. Probably because he didn't want me driving his Porsche. But I wouldn't want to learn from him anyhow because he is a terrible driver.

I'd called Alan to say I was coming and that I hoped he'd be alone. He sounded stiff. He was hurt. It was going to be hard.

But when I walked in the door, he opened his arms to me and I, hardly pausing, entered right into them. It wasn't just that he looked so handsome, it was that he looked at me with such pain and hope and gladness all mixed together that it melted my heart and made him irresistible. Plus, he was my very best friend and I'd missed him a lot. So we hugged long and happily, then he pulled away, ran to the dining room table, and began brandishing papers.

"Look! Look! It's the novel. On paper. Black and white. I've been writing every day." He tapped his head. "I told you it was all here and it is. It's going directly from my brain to my fingers. It's writing like a dream." He smiled, abashed. "Well, five pages anyhow. But it's truly begun, Jane, and I'm not going to stop until I've got it all down."

"That's wonderful Alan. I'm so glad. Congratulations."

"You were right. I was all talk and no action. It was disgusting. I don't blame you a bit for leaving me. But now I'm in high gear. You've shocked me into it. Do you want to read what I've got so far?"

The way he was waving the papers about like flag signals, I couldn't have gotten hold of them if I'd wanted to, but I didn't want to. "No thanks. Let's wait until you have a chapter."

I didn't want to jeopardize the happy moment. He was in that elated stage you experience simply because you've begun. He was happy to see me and to tell me he'd begun. My looking at what he'd written would introduce anxiety into the heady mix.

He embraced me. "You said, 'Let's wait.' That means you'll be here. You've come back to me. Oh, Jane, thank God. I've been so wretched. I've been lost without you. You're my other half. I know that now." He wiped tears from his eyes. I was touched. He was being such a human being. I felt in love all over again. We went to bed together and it was a wonderful reunion. The summer breeze blew through the bedroom windows, puffing the curtains, and the ebb and flow of ocean water was the primal background sound to our blending, a slower, louder version of our breathing. We were closer than we'd ever been. Everything was better for both of us. He had his novel under way and I had a job. Now I had to tell him about the job.

When we were up and partly dressed and in the living room, I filled him in and his face grew long.

"But, Jane, you don't need to work anymore. I'll take care of all the finances. That's no problem. I'll give you an allowance if you want, your own separate checking account. I just figured you could go to my wallet or the checkbook when you wanted to."

"I've always paid my own way. I don't like being reliant. It's an easy job. I love the kid. Like waitressing, it doesn't take any brains, so my mind is free to work on my thesis. I'll come back to you, but only with the understanding that I'm free to come and go as I please and do this job. It will be a relief to get away from all the entertaining and house guests. You know I'm not as social as you and I feel bad putting a crimp in your style."

Alan and I both sat on the couch. It was amazing how long his neck looked. He was blond and tanned and his eagle nose jutted out below blue eyes that would perhaps look icy were it not for the puppy dog eyebrows that softened them.

"But my friends love you," he said, getting up restlessly and wandering about the room. Alan was not one to sit unless he were spouting, but he was not in spouting mode and anyhow I was going to forget about the spouting. Maybe I'd imagined the spouting, along with the neck. "What do I tell them?" he asked, probably meaning his friends and certainly meaning his mother.

"That I'm working. On my thesis, if you don't want to tell them I'm a nanny. Tell them I've rented a little room of my own where I can work. You know what, Alan, maybe my being away was what you needed for your writing. People need to be alone when they work. The room I have now is perfect."

"Okay, it's weird, but I'll go along with it. No one ever said we were going to be a normal couple. But the fact is: You do work beautifully here, getting up early in the morning. Don't you?"

"Yes. It's been fine, but it's hard not to have a desk of my own. I work at the dining room table in the morning and then I have to move everything when we entertain."

"You could use one of the attic rooms."

"Oh, thanks. It's stifling up there and there are mice."

"A guest room?"

"Fine until the guests arrive. Never mind. I like this new arrangement. My writing is really on the move. You'd be surprised."

He frowned at me. "Have you gotten off the Manship thing and back to Bufano?"

Why was he starting all that again now that we'd had our nice reunion? I replied mildly, "Yes, but it didn't do any harm learning all about Manship and Hancock, now did it?"

"Hancock too."

"Yes. Hancock too. These artists are all connected. Hemingway said to learn everything about a subject, even if you only put in one sentence about it."

Frowning deeper, "But then you got hipped on the subject of quarrying itself. Surely . . ."

"Stone comes from quarries. Sculptors sculpt in stone and marble when they're not using wood or bronze or clay or . . . I have to go my own way, following my different threads. The thesis will find its shape and content somewhere inside the tangle."

I was now slightly outraged. It was one thing for me to criticize his not writing, but what right had he to criticize my writing in circles, especially after I'd relented, returned, and cheerfully embraced. That's the trouble with men. Once they've had sex, it's all back to normal, whereas with a woman the spell lingers. She feels romantic. She wants to be sweet. She doesn't want to wrangle. But, now that we were on the subject, I continued warmly.

"To me, what is so amazing about sculptors is the superhuman physical and emotional strength it takes, necessitating huge studios, endless tools, enormous expense. It is awe-inspiring. A writer just needs a piece of paper and a pen, but think what a monumental undertaking it is to be a sculptor! Benny, you know, when he found the perfect rock at a quarry in France for his St. Francis statue, built a shed around it to work in, since there was no way he could transport the rock anywhere. That was going to be a big problem too when the statue was done, but . . ."

Alan was drifting out of the room, toward the bar, and I was tagging along after him, telling him about Benny. I'd forgotten this tendency of his to wander out of earshot when I was talking, forgotten my pitiful tendency to follow him, still blabbing, even though I transparently no longer held his attention or interest.

Whereas Gled, strangely, seemed to hang on every one of my words as if they were jewels. I'd been telling him and Danny what I was learning about birds. But probably it wasn't that Gled appreciated my learning more than Alan did, it was just that birds were more interesting than sculptors.

I decided not to tell Alan I was reading about the birds of America. Even I couldn't see how they fit into my thesis about Bufano. Although everything fits together in the end. "The hip bone's connected to the tail bone" and so forth.

Bufano had statues entitled *Owl, Penguins, Duck, Parrot, Dove.* They were simple, pared-down versions. But none of them gave a feel for the fowl in the way that, say, Brancusi's masterpiece, *Bird,* did—although it was even more simplified, pared to bare bones, pared to the idea of bird. It epitomized bird in flight, made you gasp.

"Hi, Mother. Alan. Just called to say that Jane is back and all is well."

"How did you get her back?"

"It was easy. I just totally abased myself."

"Good for you. You're a son after my own heart. Your father was never able to abase himself. If only he knew how winning it is, he could have had me eating out of his hand."

"You see, the problem was that she felt I wasn't working on my novel as promised. It was, at least to her, part of our vows."

"I suppose you told her you were writing it in your head and that satisfied her for about three weeks."

"I did tell her that. And I was writing it in my head. But to her it looked like I was only playing tennis, swimming, drinking with my friends, and sleeping late in the morning."

"I can see how there might have been some confusion."

"Anyhow, I'm putting the novel on paper and we are more in love than we have ever been."

"Did she ask about the rings?"

"I forgot about the rings."

"I took them away and put them in the bank."

"Did you have a right to do that?"

"Not really. I'll recover them for you. And we must get together about the novel now that you're serious."

"Jane has gotten a place of her own to work on her thesis, so you can come by sometime when she isn't here."

"Then why can't I move back into my own house? I was letting you have it to yourselves for the honeymoon, but it sounds like the honeymoon's over and the marriage has begun."

"But you said you love the little cottage you rented for the summer."

"Did I? I forgot. What do you mean, 'a place of her own'? Why? There are ten rooms of her own in my house."

"She's taken a summer job and a room goes with it. She took the job when she thought she'd left me and now she wants to keep it. She's a nanny."

"You're kidding. What will people say?"

"They'll say I'm kidding."

{6} Repulse Mother-in-Law

One evening I returned to Alan's house from the quarry and found Alan's mother, Martha, having a drink on the porch all alone, watching the sun go down. I joined her. The porch sunsets were famous because there are not many places on the East Coast where one can see the sunset over the ocean. The reason was that the house was actually on Ipswich Bay but at such a wide part of the bay, which stretches to New Hampshire and Maine and eventually Nova Scotia, that even though there was land, the illusion was of being on open ocean. This sunset was dramatic, with swathes of red and orange sweeping across the sky against a pale yellow horizon. Returning fishing boats silhouetted themselves and a schooner belonging to the house next door crossed the path of orange on the water, all hands pulling down sails to prepare for the mooring.

We chatted idly. Martha was a woman in her late fifties and looked like Alan: slim, blonde, and blue-eyed. She maintained there had been nothing but blue eyes in her family for centuries. She must have been beautiful once, but now her face was just this side of ravaged and she didn't care. She once told me, "The great thing about having a lover your age or older is they lose their eyesight at the same rate you grow wrinkles." Another time she said, "The reason I drink so much is to forget I can't remember things anymore. What I've really forgotten is that I never had a good memory to begin with." I liked her. She was funny but not to amuse others, to amuse herself.

On this evening she asked me about my thesis, then astonished me by saying, "I wrote a story about Benny Bufano back in the early sixties. It was published in *Mademoiselle.*"

I exclaimed in wonderment and she went blithely on. "It was called 'Francis: The City, The Saint, The Statue, The Boy.' Rather an unwieldy title. It was about a boy who imagined he was St. Francis. He read in the papers about San Francisco wanting to get rid of Benny's great statue because, in its site in front of the Church of St. Francis of Assisi, the priest complained it got in the way of weddings and funerals, being so big."

"Twenty-five feet tall," I corroborated. "It was the one he made in France. And he didn't use stone cutters like other sculptors of his time. He did it all himself."

"Francis, the boy in my story, makes a pilgrimage to the city to save the statue, feeling it incumbent upon him because he has the same name as the saint."

"I'd love to see the story."

"God knows where it is." She paused and drank. "One day, on the streets of San Francisco, I ran into Benny. I shook his hand."

"*The* hand?"

"Yes, the hand he'd cut the finger off . . ."

"And sent to President Wilson to protest the war. That was

when he was only eighteen. Imagine! And he really needed that finger too."

"Some say he'd cut it off by accident and then decided to make the grand gesture for publicity. He was always a publicity hound."

"I choose to believe otherwise," I said loyally. "But why did you never tell me you were a writer?"

"I wrote under another name. Just short stories for what was known as the slicks, for the money."

"That doesn't sound in the least like a slick story."

"It was my first published story. I got slicker as I went along. Certainly, my titles were slicker." She laughed.

"All the American writers wrote for the slicks at that time. Even Salinger."

"Except that I never graduated to *The New Yorker."*

"But now Alan will carry the torch."

She smiled.

"Tell me about Benny," I asked eagerly.

"He was tiny. Elfin. Rather like Brancusi physically but nowhere near the genius."

"I disagree. I think he was near. It's funny, I was just thinking about Brancusi's *Bird* the other day. He was like Bufano, in that he was a poor boy and made his way in the world. He ran away from home when he was twelve. Benny ran away too but not before stealing two thousand dollars from his mother. He said he'd pay it back when he was famous and he did get famous, but he didn't pay it back."

"What a rat. I wonder if he knew Brancusi."

"They might have been in Paris at the same time."

"Benny didn't like anyone's work but his own. A nasty man, really. Unlike Walker Hancock, who's the nicest man who ever lived. A saint."

"I think an artist should be judged solely on his work, not on how nice he is."

"I don't. Anyhow, don't you think some of Bufano's work, his animals and birds, were sort of cute?"

I blushed. My face picked up the sunset colors. It was intolerable to think I would be doing a dissertation on an artist whose work was cute. "No, I do not," I said.

Despite disagreements, this was the best conversation I ever had with Alan's mom. She seemed to like me better now that I wasn't around so much. Not that it mattered what she thought—about me or Bufano. What mattered was that she and Alan loved each other. Because I love my mom so much, I like it when other people love theirs. It was one of the things that drew me to Alan. Other boyfriends used to hate it that I'd talk to Mom on the phone so much. Alan called his mom more than I did mine.

Darkness infiltrated the sunset. As if the night had caused a mood change, Martha turned querulous. "Alan tells me you've got a nanny job. I don't understand. It would be extremely embarrassing to the family if this got out. What's it all about? Why are you doing this?"

I said, "It's really none of your business."

She laughed appreciatively. A loon also laughed from somewhere out on the water—eerie, taunting clarinet laughter from the underworld.

Dear Janice:

Yesterday, in an attempt to get Effie's attention, I jumped out of a light plane over the quarry and parachuted down, hoping like hell I wouldn't land in a tree and remain hopelessly entangled, making an ass out of myself. I'd alerted Danny and told him to be out on the lawn with Effie at a certain time. It was perfect. I even missed the water and landed on the side lawn that leads to the bluff. I stepped blithely from my harness and said, "Anything to drink around here?"

She wasn't as excited as Danny. However, she clapped and laughed and seemed really surprised. That's good. But what'll I do for Act Two?

Love,
Gleddenning

For Act Two, you arrive at the quarry with a tall, stunning, brilliant woman—me.

See you soon,
Janice

{7} Stepping Back Too Far

The next evening I was at the quarry. Danny was at a friend's house for the night and Gled was going out after dinner, so I had the night free, but I decided not to go to the shore. I told Alan I was needed at my job. I looked forward to an evening alone with the bird book. I loved the freedom of the two lives. You'd think leading two lives would give you less time to yourself, but actually it gives you more.

I'd told Gled that I had rented a room in which to write my thesis, as I found it hard to write at the quarry, where I wanted to be with him and Danny. This explained where I went on my hours off. I didn't tell him about Alan because I'd hired myself out to Gled believing myself to be a single woman again, and so decided, since it was only for a month, to keep it that way and not get into the theater of it all.

The Flanagans were always in residence, but after dinner they retired to their own quarters, where they had a sitting room papered with pictures of progeny, as well as two small bedrooms. Once a week they went bowling and on Sundays they went to Sacred Heart and lunch with friends. They were in their seventies and very cozy, reminding me of a lot of Mom's Irish friends in Boston.

After dinner, Gled settled himself in the living room to make some phone calls before going out and I went to the bluff to do T'ai Chi. It was dusk. The quarry water was merging with the rocks and trees, but there was a wash of color in the western sky. The air was still and there were mosquitoes. It was a challenge to go through the form without slapping them away or scratching a bite. Bats were flitting through the air, doing their job of eating the insects, and also trout leapt up from the water, but the two diverse species hardly made a dent in the mosquito population. I closed my eyes to help myself ignore their existence.

The form is hard to do in darkness, since it is all a matter of equilibrium, but it is part of the practice to periodically try and do so. During Repulse Monkey, I teetered a time or two before finding my foot-plant in the backward step. I kept on, trying to perfect the moves with shuttered eyes until the moment came when I stepped back and found no ground at all on which to root my foot. There was only air. My reaching leg plunged downward and my front leg folded. My eyes flew open, but I was already falling off the cliff. I don't know if I screamed. It happened so fast and unexpectedly that, if I did scream, it was no cranelike carrying call—more like the piping of a small flummoxed night bird.

I hit the water. I went under fast. It was darker than it had been with my eyes shut. Terrified, I scrabbled my way to the surface. "Help, help!" *Glub, glub,* and under again, falling like an iron ball. Thrashing and flailing my way upward again. No idea of trying to swim. No memory of the benighted long-ago dog-paddle of my infancy.

Was this it, then? Was this to be the end? A watery grave. Would they drag the bottom for me or wait for me to swell up with gases and float to the top?

I felt a large body displacing the waters, swirling around my presently passive sinking self. For some reason I thought, "Alligator!" and recommenced my panicky flailing, trying to scream when I resurfaced but coughing and sputtering instead. All I could see were gleaming teeth. I struck out at the alligator with all my might.

"Effie, it's Gled. Calm down. Try to be still. I'm taking you in."

"Help! Help!"

"I am helping, but you have to help *me* by not struggling."

"Help!"

"I'm sorry to have to do this, Effie."

When I came to, I was naked, wrapped in a soft flannel robe, stretched out on the couch. Gled was squatting before a not-very-good fire in the fireplace, feeding it sticks, swearing under his breath.

"Where am I?" I asked. It was something I've always wanted to say.

He sprang to my side. "Effie, darling, are you all right?"

Effie, darling?

"Can I get you anything?"

"Brandy. Doesn't the drowning girl always get brandy?"

"Not nowadays. It's considered bad for hypothermia or shock."

"I'm not in shock and I'm warm and toasty." This was because of the bathrobe not the fire, which smoked and fizzled rather than flamed. "I just feel really tired and as if I've been hit in the head."

He went away and returned with a snifter of cognac, not realizing a shot glass was more my style. I slugged it down, coughing my head off afterward, and held out the snifter for more. He set the empty glass on the table and sat on the couch, taking my hands in his. "Thank God I was watching you do your T'ai Chi. I love to watch you. I watch every night. But tonight you didn't seem to know where you were or what you were doing. You were all over the place."

"Where am I?" I murmured again, loving the idea of not knowing, although of course I really did know. I remembered the moment of waking in the convertible, where, for a few seconds, I didn't know and how nice it was, how freeing.

I wanted to be free. But I was free, wasn't I? Had marriage made me feel confined? Is that why I left? If so, why had I gone back to Alan? Because Mom wanted me to? Because I loved him? Because he'd started his novel?

The brandy raced to my head. I was instantly drunk. It was good I was lying down or I'd have fallen down. It was good he hadn't refilled my glass. The fire, as if it too had partaken of cognac and was ignited thereby, began to send up flower-like flames, blurry ones.

Gled's concerned face wavered before me. "You saved my life," I told him. "Thank you."

"Oh, Effie, darling, if I lost you, I don't know what I'd do. I love you. I've loved you since the moment we met."

"But, Gled . . ."

He was caressing me. First just my face, running his hands over my face and kissing it, kissing me. But then he was loosening the robe and caressing my breasts and stomach. "But, Gled . . ."

I was too tired and drunk and surprised and sexed-up to stop him. It was affirming life. Snatched from the alligator jaws of death, the first thing one wants to do is have sex. Or is it when someone else dies that one wants to have sex? Probably one wants to have sex any time for any reason.

Gled was a bold, vigorous lover, unlike the comparatively languid Alan. He was zesty. He handled my body with authority and verve, turning me this way and that. There is a not-very-nice thing said about small women such as myself that a big man can just put her on his penis and spin her around. Gled didn't actually do that, but he sort of took me in that spirit. First he kissed me everywhere, unlike the languid and actually rather persnickety Alan.

Gled wasn't a big man, really. He was shorter than Alan. But he was thick. He was bearish. He was a bear and I was his honey pot.

I was really drunk.

We tumbled around the couch. I felt like I was in a dryer. Then I made the call of the coitus that would do a Whooping Crane proud. Talk about trumpets from the underworld. I discovered a whole new larynx.

"Oh, Effie, my dearest darling wonderful one!" He went on in this way, pulling out all the stops, free-associating, saying everything that came to mind, but it was like hearing a bedtime story. Within seconds I was asleep.

I slept until dawn, awakening beside Gled in the master suite. He was staring at me with joy in his eyes. He reached for me, but I repulsed him. Repulse employer. "Gled, no. This was all a big mistake." I jumped from the bed, but, seeing nothing to cover myself with, got back in, wrapping the sheet around me.

Gled, sensitively, got out of bed himself and walked to the adjoining bathroom, returning with two robes, one of which he was wearing. He dropped the other on the bed, then sat down on a chair.

"It's not a mistake, Effie. I love you. I want to marry you."

I was stunned, but before reacting I tried to be polite. I fell into pseudo Jane Austen-ese, saying I was sensible of the honor, and so forth, but quickly segued into Effie Crackalbee-ese. "Gled, I was all shaken up last night and full of gratitude and quite drunk from the brandy and I forgot myself."

Gled was quiet. His expression was hard to read.

"Yes, I forgot myself. I didn't know who I was or what I was doing."

I decided his expression was one of utter dejection and felt like a rat.

"Although, don't misunderstand me, I liked it. You were wonderful. You are wonderful."

He perked up a little, but I remembered it wasn't my job to perk him up; it was my job to discourage him from these fancies of his. I grew stern. "But this won't do. I'm your son's nanny and can be nothing more to you than that. I can't continue working for you in a situation like this." I gestured to the rumpled bed. "If we can somehow forget last evening and be as we were, then I'll go on with the job. Otherwise, I'll have to leave today, this minute."

He stood up. "We can be as we were, Effie, until Danny goes back to his mother and no longer needs you. But I can't forget last evening and I hope that we might, well, begin to see each other . . ."

"It is out of the question. I had better leave today."

"No, please don't." He stood up, looked at me searchingly, then turned his back to me. "Okay, we'll pretend it never happened. We both forgot ourselves and now we'll forget it. It never happened."

He walked out of the room, looking, for someone so beefy, noble. Why didn't I just tell Gled I was married? Well, I couldn't stand it that I'd misrepresented myself to him. I didn't lie, but I didn't tell. It was a lie of omission. It was a lie.

At the time, I had genuinely left Alan, unringed myself, written the goodbye letter, and to all intents and purposes wasn't married. But when I went back to Alan possibly I was wrong not to tell Gled the situation. I would have if I'd known he was having these fantasies about me.

Maybe Alan's pretending he was writing a novel was nothing to my pretending I was an unmarried woman. I'd deluded Gled, led him down the garden path, never mind that it was all-unknowing. And now, after a wonderful night, I'd kicked him in the teeth.

I didn't like the anti-Effie turn my mind was taking, making me feel so bad about myself. My self-esteem was going into a sinkhole. I turned it around fast, taking another tack.

He took advantage of me, a poor frightened, half-drowned woman, after slugging me in the head then giving me brandy, even though it was contraindicated. He seduced a young weakened woman in his employ. Typical New England aristocrat brute behavior, invoking the rights of a liege lord over his peasant nanny.

"Hi, Janice. It's Gled."

"What's wrong, little brother?"

"I asked her to marry me and she said no."

"Oh, Gled!"

"I know."

"No, you don't know because what I'm 'Oh, Gledding' about is that I feel like you've gone crazy. You've only known the girl two weeks."

"If you could meet her, you'd see why."

"Maybe I'd better. I'll come for a visit. I want to see Danny and there's also a writer I need to meet with."

"But she turned me down, Janice. She's only staying on if we forget the whole thing."

"What whole thing?"

"Well, last night she fell into the quarry and I saved her life and in the emotion of it all, we made love. This morning she says it was a big mistake and to forget it ever happened and she'll only stay on under those conditions."

"I wonder what her game is."

"She has no game. She just wants to support herself while she writes her thesis."

"You're an attractive man, a sweetheart, with the most beautiful home on earth, an adorable son, and she says forget about it? Maybe she doesn't know what a do-gooder you are and thinks you're a rich playboy. Did you tell her you fly medical supplies to God-forsaken outposts of the Americas?"

"I told her a little about it. But never mind that. The sex, Janice. I could tell the way her body responded to me that there's love there. It was so . . ."

"I'm not interested in details, Gledass. Sex is sex. It doesn't mean a thing. You've always made too much of it. How was it with your wife?"

"Wonderful, actually."

"Well, there you are."

"Where am I?"

{8} Golden Pheasant Stands on One Leg

Speaking of birds, Golden Pheasant Stand on One Leg is the T'ai Chi posture in which you stand on your left leg and lift your right leg with knee bent, toes down. Your right elbow rests on the knee, with arm and hand perpendicular. Your left arm is down, open hand resting lightly against your left thigh. You come into this position from a squatting down posture.

Birds of America hasn't much to say about the pheasant because it isn't an American bird. It was introduced here from Europe and China. The Golden Pheasant is from the mountains of eastern Tibet.

I have fallen into a funk since the drowning episode, although I force myself to be cheerful with Danny, who's the best little boy in the whole world.

What I should do is go and talk with my thesis adviser. I have become disheartened with Benny. "The fact is," I told my mom on the phone, "the man was a louse with women. The woman he got pregnant and took to San Francisco, he never acknowledged as a wife and lived with secretly, pretending to others he was a single man. He never acknowledged the child as his either. Later he married a lovely young San Francisco girl from a good family, not telling her about the first 'wife.' They went to Europe together, then he dumped her, sending her home pregnant, never acknowledging that child as his either. He never helped these women financially.

"Mom, do I want to spend years writing about this man? I admire his total commitment to his art, that he was a poor boy who came up from nowhere with the help of no one, no grants, no universities. He struggled. He worked his ass off. He went to China, for God's sake, and lived on rice. I love all that about him. But he was a liar and a shithead, really. I think a man's art is what is important, not the personality of the man who created it, but can you separate the two? Aren't a man's heart and soul going to inform his art? This is a big question, worth writing a thesis about, except there is no answer, at least not from such a one as I."

"Effie, honey, I have to say that I think you are feeling troubled about yourself and you are laying it all on Benny. You knew all this about him before. Why is it troubling you now?"

"It's true, Mom. A month ago I thought I was so great. I've always thought I was great."

"You are great, Effie."

"That's why it was so easy to judge Alan, from the height of my own hardworking perfection and integrity. Now I am feeling a tiny bit flawed."

"That's okay, Effie. It will make you deeper and your thesis will come out even better. Life isn't all book learning after all or looking at art for hours at a time. It's understanding what makes us all tick, right? This guy, Benny, put his art before his personal relationships. Maybe that wasn't so nice. But maybe he had to make it his first priority. He had lofty ideas. He wanted to stay centered. He was unable to take on the responsibility of wife and kids. In those days women didn't work, you know. The man shouldered all the financial burden. What about the French? Think about them."

"The French? Right. All those French painters and sculptors were impregnating women right and left and none of the art historians cared. They didn't even know their names unless they were models, then they might know their nicknames. They thought of them as loose women honored to have the great man stick his cock in. But they weren't honored. They were stuck with a child to raise and no help and getting older and fatter and . . ."

"Did you ever think maybe they had fun? Women like sex too, you know. Maybe the artists talked really nice to them at the same time, made them feel beautiful, special, wanted."

Mom was talking about herself now, her and her lawyers. It made me feel sad. I told her goodbye for now and thanks. Then I went and told Danny about hummingbirds.

"Their wings beat ninety times a second."

More than twice as fast when they're courting, but I decided not to get into all that.

"A second! That sounds impossible."

We were walking down High Street to the village, Danny carrying his skateboard until we got to the smooth macadam. It was like an extension of his arm. He didn't even think about it. We both wore baggy shorts and T-shirts, our bathing suits underneath. It was hot. Danny had a baseball cap, but I didn't.

"But wait until you hear this! It's only four inches long and migrates almost two thousand miles, crossing six hundred miles of water! That's what I don't get. A bird that has to eat twice its weight every day flies six hundred miles nonstop. It's the miracle of the ages."

"Probably it prepares by fattening up, like bears do before they go to their dens for the winter. But still! All those wing beats! What's ninety beats a second times six hundred miles?"

"We'd have to know how long it takes him to cross the water, not how many miles it is."

Danny paused. "Let's go look in here."

We were passing the community garden. We stepped off the road into a wonderland of sunflowers, cosmos, corn, and tomatoes, everything growing higher than our heads. Around the quarry Gled just allowed the indigenous ferns and wildflowers: the Queen Anne's lace, goldenrod, and purple loosestrife. In the community garden we saw a Ruby-Throated Hummingbird, as if we'd conjured him up. No Golden Pheasants. There was a Cardinal, pure red, perching on the head of a sunflower. The colors took my breath away. This was art. This was the real thing.

We rounded a corn corner and came upon a very old man, standing still, leaning on a cane, watching the flash-away flight of the Cardinal. He was dressed neatly in crisp khakis and blue shirt and wore a short-brimmed cap. He looked our way and smiled gently. I felt in the presence of someone wonderful.

"Hello, Mr. Hancock," Danny said.

"Hello, Danny."

He and Danny chatted. I hung back, standing on one foot with the other foot wrapped around the ankle, very unbirdlike. Hanging back position. Hands behind me, one holding the wrist of the other, just as one foot held the other's ankle. Wings pinned back. Not a T'ai Chi posture. Thesis writer humbled in the presence of great sculptor posture—but keeping her balance.

Danny and I walked on down High Street. "He's so nice," Danny said.

"He's ninety years old," I said. It was as if I were telling another hummingbird fact. It was as if I were telling how many teeth he had.

Danny, rightly, reprovingly, said, "So what." Putting down

his board, he pushed off, having finally come to civilization, ergo: pavement, curbs to jump up on, steps to bump down, railings to ride, and walls to jump on or over, his board, against all the laws of gravity, cleaving to his feet.

"Look out for cars! Be careful!" I shouted after him but not too worriedly because Danny was careful and alert and there weren't many cars on this street. Still, I walked faster, then began to trot to keep him in sight.

Danny and I waited for a car to pass before crossing the main street to go into the village store. It was my mother-in-law, Martha. She waved.

We went to the store and bought grape Popsicles, which we slurped down before the sun could melt them as we walked down to Lanes Cove, my favorite place. The luminous cove water was separated from Ipswich Bay by a silver-gray granite breakwater. Lobstermen's dories and fishing boats lay on the water, stacks of wooden lobster pots stood on the pier, shingled cottages and tarpaper shacks lined one side, and, as always, an artist had set up her easel in the weave of grasses and wildflowers and was happily painting away, protected by a large straw hat I lusted after. It was so hot I felt as though my hair was on fire.

We walked out on the top of the breakwater in search of a breeze. "A hundred years ago," I told Danny, "the air would be periodically shattered by blasting from the quarries. Rocks turned into paving stones would be carted down from your quarry, Devil's Rock, and Walker Hancock's Deep Hole and loaded onto three-masted schooners here in the cove. The schooners would sail off with them to pave the streets of Philadelphia."

"Do hummingbirds ever walk?" Danny asked, sitting down and dangling his legs over the edge. Out on the bay a filigree of gulls followed a fishing boat for about half a mile, thinning out to a solitary gull at the end.

"They can perch. They can cling. But they're the only bird

that can't walk. They might be the only bird that can fly upside down and backward. They can also hover."

"What's 'hover'?"

"Just hang the air."

"Effie, how come you know so much stuff?"

"I'm an obsessive reader and I have a memory that won't stand still."

"My dad's like a bird."

"Right. He lives in the sky a lot of the time."

"Yeah, but also he used to be a parachutist. Not for the war. He did it to compete. He'd jump out of a plane with a bunch of guys and make designs in the sky while he was falling. Then they'd open their chutes at the last minute."

"Wow."

"He won lots of prizes. His team was one of the best in the world. But Mom was always so scared all the time. Finally she just couldn't stand being married to him anymore."

"That's too bad."

"I know you have to be careful sometimes, but I don't think you should go around being scared. Do you love my dad?"

I flushed even hotter than I already was. "I think he's a very nice man. Come on. Let's walk along the rocks to Pebble Cove and have a swim. I want you to teach me not to sink."

"I'll teach you the dead-man's float," he said happily.

{9} Standing on No Legs

"Alan? It's your mother."

"Hi."

"I just saw Effie with a little boy. So it's true. She really is a nanny."

"Of course she is. I never doubted it for a minute."

"She looked like a little boy herself. She looked happy."

"That's good."

"He had a skateboard."

"Mom, why are you dwelling on this vision of Effie?"

"I don't know. She looked so . . . out of context. It was like discovering her in another life."

"Well, she's not leading a secret life, is she? Since I know all about it. You're the secret-life-leader. Can I tell Effie, by the way? She's family now."

"I wouldn't. She might think I'm writing your novel for you."

"No, she won't. Anyhow, you're just editing it. It's my story."

"That's what they all say."

Shortly after I got to the shore house that evening, Alan returned home with three fellow tennis players I hadn't met before. They were all thirsty and ravenous and kept asking me to get things for them. I retired early. When Alan joined me, I said I didn't want to make love and he was amenable to having a conversation instead. That's when he told me about his mother.

"Mom's a ghostwriter," he said out of the blue. He was smoking, which I hate, and there were wreaths of pollution above the bed. He was lying flat on his back and blowing it this way and that, as if creating, not wrecking, the atmosphere.

"Movie stars' biographies? Stuff like that?"

"No. She's unique." Alan spoke with admiration. "Say some young writer has a smashing success and the onus is on him or her to come up with a second novel and he's given a gigantic advance, but he can't perform. He chokes. So Mom writes it. She studies his style. She gets to know him, his life, his vision of life, his experiences, and goes ahead and writes the hell out of it. Or it might be a well-known writer who's blocked and everyone's going to forget about him if he doesn't come up with a new book soon. Same thing. She writes it for him and gets the second half of the advance. He's already spent the first half."

"Then she and the writer are defrauding the publisher?"

"But you see . . ." He held up a finger as he did when making a surprise point in class. "It's the publisher who hires her."

"Then the reading public is being defrauded," I said grumpily, refusing to admire criminal behavior, even if it was his mother's. "They're buying a forgery."

"But they've only paid twenty-five bucks and they're getting a good read. What about all these massive novels people buy because the research is so great. The writer didn't do the research. He hired it out and it came into his novel via modem, pages and pages of the stuff."

"That's different from creative writing."

"In the art world, a museum might pay millions for a fake Van Gogh. Then the museum and public are being defrauded big-time."

"So you're saying forgery's okay, as long as it's twenty-five dollars, not a million."

He stubbed out his vile cigarette. "Actually, I've always thought that if it's as good as Van Gogh did it and everyone loves it, who cares? Van Gogh's dead, so he doesn't care. I think forgery is okay if it's as good as the real thing."

"It's not okay because a copy is not art. It is not informed by genius. A clever person can copy Hemingway's style, but he isn't Hemingway. He didn't put in the years of dedication and commitment to become the unique writer . . ."

Alan interrupted and argued on for the sake of argument, not because he believed what he was saying. He spouted. He got up and walked around the room. He raised his finger a lot. I wanted to scream.

Finally I burst in. "The art world is rotten to the core. And money's what's made it so. Alan, I'm thinking of changing my discipline."

"What?" He got back into bed, leaned against the headboard, and looked at me.

"I've lost interest in my thesis." Saying it made me want to cry.

"That's natural," he said breezily, waving my angst aside. "It will pass. When I was writing my . . ."

"I want to be an ornithologist."

He laughed. "You found some old book about birds, right? Ha ha ha." He rolled around the bed laughing his head off.

"Well, at least you didn't decide to be a quarrier when you were reading about quarrying. We can be glad of that." He laughed some more. "You haven't the build for it."

"I'm serious, Alan. I had an epiphany in the community garden today . . ."

He looked interested but not in my epiphany. In the garden. "I didn't know Lanesville had a community garden and I've summered here all my life."

"I saw a Cardinal on a sunflower," I pressed on. "Oh, the colors! The life and the beauty. The wonder of it all. I never felt that way about art. I only thought I did, but today when . . ."

"Where is the garden located exactly?"

"Never mind the damn garden. Listen to me. Art history is fusty and musty. It's all indoors. And it's full of forgery. Whereas each bird is the real thing."

He frowned at me. "This is a crazy idea. A passing fancy. It makes no sense. You're a city girl who's never shown the slightest interest in nature. Ornithologists don't make any money. They don't teach at universities. It requires endless patience and incredibly keen eyesight. You haven't a leg to stand on."

I was hurt and fell silent. He relented, giving me permission to be interested in birds. "Okay, go ahead and watch birds, but just think of it as a nice hobby, an antidote to the real work of your life. I'll buy you some binoculars."

"I hate Benny Bufano."

"I'm going to sleep." He turned his back to me, wriggled into a comfortable position, and subsided.

"Anyhow, I don't need a leg to stand on. I learned to float today. Danny taught me."

Alan snored. It was probably a fake snore to show his total disinterest in me, my epiphanies, my swimming, and my career—although he did have the gift of instant sleep. I talked on. "And the hummingbird doesn't need a leg to stand on either because it's an aerialist and wing-beater *par excellence.* It can fly nonstop six hundred miles. Do you know it's eensy nest is made of dandelion fluff and lichen, held together by spiderweb, lined with down? Doesn't it sound like a fairy nest?"

Alan was snoring in earnest, so I ceased talking aloud, thinking to myself that if I were an ornithologist, I could spend my life looking at birds, watching their behavior, and memorizing fascinating facts about them. I'd never have to think about my life at all because that would be my life. And Danny could come with me.

{10} Taking the Cake

Taking the cake is not a T'ai Chi posture. It was what Alan flung at me the next morning as I was leaving for work. "You take the cake!" It means: "You're the limit. You've gone too far this time. You disgust me. I've had it with you. You're the prime example of what we're talking about."

I believe those are the sorts of things it means, but I'm not sure where it comes from.

I had done my T'ai Chi, eaten my cereal with berries, drunk my coffee, and was about to depart for my job when I thought I'd write Alan a note. I was just putting it on his bedside table when he opened his eyes and said dryly, "I suppose you're leaving me again because I don't think you should throw away your Harvard education to become a bird-watcher."

"No. I was thinking about . . ."

He sat up, interrupting as usual. I looked at my watch. There wasn't time for a spout or even a burble. "I've been thinking too," he said, "I hardly slept during the night."

Untrue.

"You've turned against Benny, just like you turned against

me a few weeks ago, for no reason, except that he and I didn't come up to some expectation of perfection that you had in mind for us."

I said honestly, "That could be."

His anger was deflated. "It's because you start out overenthusiastic. You're bound to be disappointed."

"You're right. Mom thinks it's that I get unhappy with myself and put it on the other person for letting me down in some way, even though it's I who have let myself down."

"That's a good explanation too. Because when you thought you were upset with me for not writing my novel, you were actually upset with yourself for wandering in your thesis."

"I wasn't wandering," I said firmly. "I was enlarging my exploration. I was damned upset with you for the good reason that your novel was hot air."

"Let me see the note."

"What note?"

"The note you've written me."

I crumpled it and stuck it in my jeans pocket. "It's about your mother."

"I suppose I misrepresented myself to you because I didn't tell you my mother was a ghostwriter before we were married." He laughed. "Grounds for divorce: ghostwriter mother."

"She's a forger. I'm sure she'd say so herself. Now I understand why she was always suspecting me of foul play or crediting me with an unsavory past. It's because she herself is the outlaw. They say you don't look behind doors unless you've stood behind them yourself."

"What she is doing is neither a felony nor a misdemeanor," he said haughtily. "It is simply a business practice."

"Which is known in the argot as white-collar crime."

"Good. Go ahead and leave me, then."

"You should be with someone tall and blond anyway," I

said. "Your friends think I'm the maid because I'm dark and short."

"So that's what this is really about." He laughed delightedly.

"No, it isn't," I said, going out the door. "It's about your mother's hanky panky and your admiration of it."

"You take the cake!" he shouted after me.

It was a windy day and the air pulled at my hair. On Ipswich Bay the water was whitecapped and noisy. I clambered up the rocky ledge in back of the house, so I could grab a few wild blueberries en route: tiny, succulent, with a gray blush over the blue. The moss around the bushes was thick and spongy with morning dew. The other higher bushes were poison sumac with red velvet blossoms shaped like pinecones. I'd always loved nature. Why didn't Alan know that about me? Boston had plenty of nature right on the Commonwealth Avenue center strip, not to mention Arnold Arboretum. But if I told him that, he'd just say, "Where exactly is Arnold Arboretum?"

I walked down the shore road, crossed over at Sacred Heart, and started up High Street. Here the air was calm and I began to feel the heat. Birds were singing, but I didn't know what kinds of birds. Maybe I never would. A shrill sound betokening Alan's Porsche drowned out the aerial melodies. He screeched to a stop beside me. As always, I wondered how one so gentlemanly and graceful on his feet could be, on wheels, so loud, clumsy, and attention-getting. Gled, being a pilot, drove unerringly—so well you didn't notice his driving at all and felt safe and trusting. You might have been home in an armchair, even if he was going eighty.

"I'll give you a ride to work," Alan said. It was thoughtful of him and I was touched. It was so out of character. It must have cost him. I envisioned him jumping out of bed, pulling on his shorts and T-shirt, dashing to the car, all of which actions were anathema to his normal languor.

But I didn't want a ride. I didn't want my two lives to touch, let alone merge. I wanted my own feet to be the connection to the two houses. It was like a room of my own, only it was a road of my own. Alan was a summer shore person. He didn't belong inland. It was not his territory. The quarries belonged to me. Gled and Danny were mine too. Mine alone.

"I want to walk," I told him gently. "I want to think. Thank you, though. It was nice of you to offer."

"Come on. Get in the car. I want to be with you. I never see you. You're never home."

"I was home at six o'clock last night. You came in at eight with your friends, who thought I was the maid."

Alan laughed again.

"I forgot to tell you that Heedless and Needless called yesterday," he said, one amusing thought leading to another. "They want to come down for the weekend."

Those were his names for my sisters. He knew it angered me to hear him call them that, although I had to admit the names were sadly fitting. He thought it was funny and my reaction was what amused him most.

"I'll call them," I said easily, not reacting as he'd expected. I stepped away from the car. "Have a good day writing." He looked at me quizzically, shifted into first, then burned rubber down High Street, rounding the corner to take the turn toward the village.

He was out of sight when I heard, "Slow down! Jerk!" I recognized Gled's voice, although I'd never heard him angry, never heard his voice raised. I found myself blushing for Alan, who was probably giving Gled the finger in retaliation—again, something he'd never do, except from his car.

I strode on down the road of my own and in a moment Gled pulled up beside me in his yellow Ford convertible. Danny was with him, which is probably why he'd yelled, "Jerk!" instead of the more appropriate "Asshole!"

I hadn't had a lot of interaction with Gled since our big night, but when I did he was as nice as ever. He had kept his promise about forgetting what had happened and going on as usual. I, however, was having a little problem. I sometimes wanted to touch him. A couple of times, during my night rambles through the house, I found myself by his bedroom door. I knew how happily I would be received if I stepped in. I don't know why I was feeling this strong temptation. I loved Alan. He was my husband. We were back together. Maybe not perfectly happy, but we understood each other. My lovemaking with Gled had been an accident, but another time it wouldn't be; it would be intentional and I would be a lowdown cheat. It was bad enough to be a disheartened nonwriting thesis writer. I didn't want to be a cheat besides.

He pulled the car up beside me. "We're off to the airport to get my sister."

Danny was looking sullen. I smiled at him. "Does Danny want to stay with me?"

"Yes, he does, but I want him to come. It will make Janice happy."

Danny scowled. "She doesn't even know me."

"But she wants to know you. That's the whole idea. She's your aunt."

"She's mean. You said she was mean to you when you were little."

"Of course she was. All older brothers and sisters are mean. They're supposed to be. It's their job. That's why I didn't give you an older sibling—so you wouldn't suffer at his or her hands. Or a younger sibling to suffer at your hands."

Danny perked up. "But I want a younger brother. I really do. But not a sibling exactly."

I loved these conversations between the two of them and listened avidly. Gled always talked about real things. Alan was hot air. Yes, I was back to thinking he was hot air. And when he wasn't spouting, he was just making fun of everything, especially me. I guess I used to think he was witty. Maybe I even used to laugh at his names for my sisters. Alan was heartless and Gled was a human being.

But what was the good of trashing Alan in my mind and honoring Gled? What about me? What was I?

"Effie? Are you all right?"

"No. I . . . I'm having trouble with my thesis."

"I'm sorry."

My hand was holding the top of the car door. He put his hand over mine. He did it without thinking, just because he felt sorry about my trouble. I had to pull my hand away. I had to. His face reddened. He put the car in gear and looked straight ahead. "We'll be back in time for lunch."

"Bye, Effie," Danny called. "Bye!"

I take the cake.

When I came to the split in the road that divided the driveways of Gled and Walker Hancock, I took Hancock's. It was not a big deal. Although the two roads diverged in the woods, neither was the road less travelled; they were both just driveways. I was curious to see Hancock's quarry, so I trespassed.

His house and studio together were much smaller than Gled's house and made of stone instead of wood. They looked timeless. I felt I could be standing anywhere in the world, any secret place, and that it could be any century. While Gled had a great spread of green lawn around his house, keeping the woods at a remove, the sculptor's buildings were in the forest. I must have been standing on a rise because beyond the calm quarry water surrounded by rose-brown rock, I could see the ocean. Here inland and shore combined in one image. It startled me.

"You must be Effie. Gled told me you might be coming by." Mr. Hancock walked slowly across from his studio.

"I'm sorry for not calling first."

"Sit down." He gestured with his cane to two common white plastic chairs near the water.

"What color do you call the stone around your quarry?" I asked him.

"I don't call it a color. I say to myself it is tawny."

He told me about buying the quarry in the thirties. "I never dreamed I could own such a place," he said, his face full of wonder, even after sixty years. "It was like buying the Grand Canyon. But a friend told me it was for sale, so I went to see the old man who owned it. He wanted fifteen hundred dollars. I'd just sold a sculpture for that exact sum, so I bought it. It had always been the town swimming hole and for many years I allowed the boys to continue to use it. But the time came when people grew litigious and I was afraid to be sued for a stubbed toe."

We talked for almost an hour and he was wonderfully available. He took me to his studio and I saw a part of the great monument to World War II soldiers that stands in the Philadelphia Thirtieth Street Station. An angel is bearing a dead soldier to heaven. I asked who the model had been and he told me he tried to make the soldier's face a composite of many races.

Being with this man in his studio was one of the great moments of my life so far, not the happy sunflower epiphany of yesterday but a solemn feeling of being with a good man, an ancient, who had spent a meaningful life and who seemed wholly without ego, a man at peace with himself. His wife was dead. His one child was still alive and he'd mentioned a sister, but he seemed to be for the most part alone in his greatness and great age.

At the same time, I felt sad because I should have been

inspired, but I wasn't. I didn't care. I didn't care about art anymore. It wasn't life. It wasn't a bird.

"Alan, darling."

"Hi, Mom."

"How's the novel coming?"

"I've got thirty pages. It's beginning to have heft. It's a pleasure to carry it from room to room."

"I never heard of a novelist doing that. And, believe me, I know everything about novelists."

"What are you working on now?"

"A boring posthumous work they want me to finish. They should just be glad she's dead and they don't have to publish her anymore. However, my agent's coming to town. She has something else for me. Any news?"

"Yes. Jane threatened to leave me again when I told her your trade. She thinks you're a crook."

"But, darling, I am a crook."

"That's what she said you'd say."

"Jane and I understand each other."

"Now she wants to drop her thesis and become a bird-watcher."

"Really? How delightful. I understand. She's struggling to navigate out of the safe little academic course she's set for herself. She wants to live, to burst with the juices of life, instead of drying up like an autumn leaf."

"Like I am."

"Like you would have if you hadn't dared to write a novel. Which, mind you, it's thanks to Jane you did."

"I intended all along to write this novel. It was all in my head."

"Yes, dear. Tell me more about Jane's bird-watching."

"She saw a Cardinal on a sunflower."

"That would do it. Just the thought of it makes me want to be a bird-watcher too. Ha! Don't sound so gloomy about it. I think it's great. You and Jane are both spreading your wings."

{11} Snake Creeps Down

Regarding Snake Creeps Down, Yang Shau-hou said that his grandfather, when doing this part of the form, could pick up a coin from the ground with his mouth. The man was flexible as hell. I never saw Yang Shau-hou's grandfather do it, but I did see a video of Cheng Man-ch'ing doing the posture when he was about seventy years old and I can't even come close. I can't achieve any of the moves with his wisdom and grace, but this one I can't even physically achieve. He is squatting down on his right leg, virtually sitting on his heel, and the left leg is straight out. The right arm, for stability, is extended in hooked-hand position, while the left makes a delightful palm-out gesture to his left foot. It is done in a gliding motion that merges into Golden Pheasant Stands on One Leg. I can do it, but I can't get as far down. If I could, I'm almost certain I couldn't get up again on one leg. Or at all. As well as the video, I have a still photo that I've studied until the cows come home, perhaps thinking if I imprint it on my brain, my body will get the picture. My teacher tells me it doesn't matter how far down I creep, but having it not matter is as hard on my mind as trying to accomplish it is on my body.

Practice, Effie. Do the form. And not mind.

But I am a person who minds, to whom things matter a lot and, at this point in my life, that's the way I want it. I want to care terribly about things.

Tao Cheng, an eleventh-century Taoist scholar, says, "Of all the elements, the sage [T'ai Chi Ch'uan student] should take water as his preceptor. The sage [T'ai Chi Ch'uan student] who makes himself as water is distinguished for his humility, he embraces passivity, acts from nonaction, and conquers the world."

This does not describe Effie Crackalbee—a minder, one who acts out, an arrogant, headstrong woman who takes stone as her preceptor. A snake who stomps instead of creeps. Instead of sliding over rocks, earth, and trees like water, she crashes through the underbrush, crushing all in her path, alerting everyone to her approach, overminding and mindless, heedless and needless.

That's me. But I am practicing to be like water for when the day comes when I won't mind about things so much, when I'm fifty.

That's why I felt so alarmed at not caring anymore about the love of my life, art, and the second love of my life, Alan. Did this notcaring mean the day already had come to take the water route? Or was I noncaring and nonattached because I was depressed? I think I was depressed.

I began to think again of my ever-beckoning bedroom back home on Commonwealth Avenue and of creeping down under the covers for a night or a month. It was very alluring.

I was doing all this pondering at the village coffee shop, the very place whence, a month previously, I'd set off for the West Coast of America, getting a ride to Rockport from the very same old lady who was sitting next to me at the counter now, not talking.

Through the small window at the end of the shop, I could see Lanes Cove and it cheered me to remember my happy day there with Danny, the day he taught me to float, the day before the Gorgon came.

I was hiding out from Alan, Gled, Danny, but especially from Gled's sister, Janice, who, a week later, was still visiting and whom I hated with all my heart. She made Benny Bufano seem like an angel. She had completely taken over the quarry and dominated Gled, Danny, me, and the Flanagans with an iron hand. She treated me like the nanny I was, but since Gled and Danny had treated me more like a family member, it was hard, not to say humiliating, to be constantly told, "Do this, do that," and then be corrected when I did it badly. It was like Alan's friends treating me like the maid, only worse. Or maybe it wasn't worse because at least she didn't hit on me like they did. Or maybe it was worse because when a man comes on to you, he at least makes himself nice, even though he's ordering you around at the same time. As a servant, you're supposed to be thrilled when the gentry is attracted to you. It used to happen all the time when I was waitressing. They're giving you orders and flirting at the same time and you're in a position where you have to be pleasant, even though you want to slap their face and twist their balls. And they'll flirt right in front of their wife or girlfriend! They honestly seem to think it's part of the waitress's job to be all charmed by them and stroke their ego while taking their fucking order and carrying their bone-crushing tray full of dishes. It's the inherent threat of a lesser tip too that they're wielding.

Also, I think I'm pregnant.

Just then the hated one, sister Janice, came into the coffee shop. There was no safe haven. "Ah, working hard on your thesis, I see. She slipped onto the stool beside me—the one that wasn't occupied by the silent old lady who had once said, "Man in a hat."

It chilled me to be sitting next to Janice. It was too close to meanness. Crane huddles. Snake writhes. Golden Pheasant falls down. Repulse employer's sister if you possibly can. Good luck.

"Funny, I always think of thesis writers using a computer or at least a typewriter and using eight-and-a-half-by-eleven paper, whereas you hand-write yours in a little notebook."

I put my journal away in my purse. Now that she'd seen it, she wouldn't rest until she got her hands on it. However, it was in shorthand, something my mother had taught me and almost no one knows anymore. It looks mystifying and lovely as well as arcane.

"And where's this famous room you rent in which to work on your famous thesis? Or is this it?" She gestured around the tiny shop. "If so, I wonder where it is you spend your nights away from the quarry?" She leered.

She'd actually tried to follow me a time or two but without success, since I walked. I could easily outwalk her, and you can hardly follow a walker in a car, at least not unbeknownst to the walker.

"Fuck off." It was something I'd never said to anyone before and it was a real pleasure. I felt free to express myself, since I had only a few more days at Gled's anyhow. Danny was going back to his mother, who had probably divorced Gled because of his sister.

"Good." She smiled. She had Gled's teeth. "Showing your true colors at last. Well, let's talk. Cards on the table. I know you seduced Gled. I know he's crazy about you and that he asked you to marry him."

"Do you know I said no?"

"Yes. Smart. He'd have tired of you in a few days otherwise. This way he's fascinated and meanwhile you work on Danny, worm your way into his heart."

"What *is* your problem?" Her nastiness really amazed me.

"I'm looking out for my little brother. He got burned by Danny's mother, emotionally and financially. You might as well know he has no money to speak of after paying alimony and child support. His dumb piloting job is virtually charity and barely pays for the gas. Don't be misled by the family home, which belongs to both of us but which I pay the taxes on, since my salary is in six figures."

"Let me guess. You're a lawyer."

"Yes, I am a lawyer, but my profession is literary agent."

"So what are you afraid of, that your brother will find happiness at last?"

"I'm afraid of little fortune hunters like you coming and taking him for the bit of money he has left."

"Oh, grow up." I stood, leaving money on the counter, overtipping in the way that every ex-waitress does. "Get a life. Get a heart first." She brought out the mundane in me. Everything I'd said since she sat down was common, tiresome, and paltry English, not befitting a near doctor of fine arts, not even befitting a little fortune hunter.

Little was the key word here. Except for my sisters and Mom and my two close friends from school—and maybe Alan's mother—women don't like me and it's mostly because I am thin and little. My figure is perfect and I have to admit my features are too, but it is the littleness that seems to peeve women most. Especially big women like Janice—although she was stunning and had nothing to worry about on that score. On the personality score she was in big trouble. She should go to prison for that personality. She should be in solitary.

I turned to go.

"By the way, you're fired, you little bitch" (*little* being the key word).

"I'm on my way to pack and go."

I was, but first I was taking the bus to Gloucester town to go to the drugstore and buy a home pregnancy test. Snake slithers away as fast as she can.

While waiting at the bus stop, I saw Martha go into the coffee shop and be embraced by Janice and realized that Janice must be the conniving literary agent of the fraudulent writer. It figured.

{12} Snake Coils Up

"Effie, honey, Alan's on the phone again. Won't you speak to him? He says why don't we all come down for the weekend. I'd love it. So would your sisters. This heat. It's hell on earth."

"Okay," I said limply. It was easier to say yes. The weekend was far away. It was only Wednesday. I snuggled deeper under the covers, even though the apartment was hellishly hot, because why be in bed and not under the actual beddy-clothes, where the healing was and the comfort and the eventual return to a state of merriness.

Mom lit up. "Will you tell him so yourself?"

"No, tell him I'm sick in bed and can't talk."

"I've told him that every day. He wants to know sick with what. He says it's mental, that you're having a crisis about your work. Is that right?"

"Did he tell you I was wandering in my thesis?"

"No, that was last time you left him he told me that."

"I haven't left him exactly," I said and fell silent, closed my eyes. I loved being in bed. My old bed. Single bed. All alone. Mom hovering. Bliss. I heard her return to the phone.

"She says we'll all come down this weekend, Alan. I think she just needs a little home time. She got fired from her job, you know. You didn't? Yes. I think it hurt her feelings. She loved the little boy. See you soon, then. Goodbye. Yes, I'm sure she'll call you soon. Bye."

"Did he say I got fired because I was wandering in my child care?"

"Oh, Effie, give the man a break. Sit up now and talk to me."

I didn't want to sit up. I wanted her to bustle about and plump my pillows and bring me stuff, but she was losing patience. She'd had it with me. "You've been here four days and you don't get out of bed except to go to the bathroom," she said grumpily. "The next thing will be bed pans. It's not healthy. You're not even doing your T'ai Chi. Your muscles are going to atrophy. You can get sick from lying down too long, you know," she said direly. "The body doesn't like it."

The phone rang again and she hustled off to it. It was still on the hall table, where it had been forever, with no chair by it. I'd tried to get her to buy a cordless, but she refused. She didn't like the telephone to rule, thought it should know its place: hall table.

"It's your employer," she said respectfully and meaningfully. One doesn't have to get out of bed for one's husband, but one's employer . . . Yes. Even if you're fired. Especially if you're fired because it might mean you're rehired.

"Gled? But how . . . ?" I was getting out of bed, moving autonomically. I was going to the phone. "How did you know my number?" I asked without even saying hello.

"I got it off my phone bill, which just came this morning. It was the only number you called. "Did you leave us because I offended you in some way, went back on our bargain. I know I was wrong to put my hand on yours the other day. I've been so careful . . ."

"Your sister fired me."

"I didn't know. Janice had no right. She worries about me too much. She's more like a mother than a sister. I'm sorry. We miss you so much."

"My time was almost up anyhow. I did say goodbye to Danny. Didn't Danny tell you?"

"Yes, but he didn't understand either, why you left so suddenly. We want you to come back and stay forever."

"But isn't Danny back with his mother now?"

"Yes. I guess I'm mainly speaking for myself. Now that you're no longer the nanny, I can speak my mind and heart. Come back. Marry me. I love you. Give us a chance."

"Gled . . ."

"Don't answer. I'm coming over."

"Here? How?"

"I'm right across the street at The Harvard Club. See you in two minutes. Goodbye."

I staggered back to my room, shut the door, and crawled into bed, coiling up under the covers. Mom would tell him I was sick in bed. Bless Mom. I closed my eyes.

Traitor. She let him in. She let him in my bedroom. What was she thinking to let an employer into one's own bedroom? Probably she let employers into her own a lot when we were young and at school—although God forbid a lawyer would fuck her on company time and lose some billable hours.

Gled walked in and sat on the bed. All he could see of me was snarly hair and puffy eyes, but the sight didn't dampen his ardor. Gently, he pulled down the sheet and exposed my face. He kissed me sweetly. "Will you marry me, Effie?"

I started to cry. I cried my heart out. Finally I wrested the words from where they'd been under lock and key, bolts and chains. I set them free. I guess they needed the lubrication of tears to release them. "I'm pregnant," I told him, blubbering. "I'm going to have a baby."

"Effie! That's wonderful! How amazing!" He stood up and spread his arms. He actually twirled around the room, despite its small confines, containing as it did my single bed and my sister's bunk beds, three bureaus, two side tables, and, I'm embarrassed to relate, wedding chests wherein my sisters were socking away embroidered linen for the big day, as if they were living at the turn of the century. "Danny's little brother is coming!" he shouted.

Seeing him so happy made me cry harder. "I'm not sure he's yours, Gled. I'm just not sure."

His face fell a mile. He sat back down on the bed, looking stunned. "There's someone else?"

I nodded, gulping, wiping my eyes and nose on the sheet.

"Of course there's someone else," he spoke to himself. "A beautiful young woman like you. Why did I never suppose there was someone else? It explains everything." He was quiet a long moment. "Of course," he said again. "What an idiot I am." He got up and turned to walk out of the room but, by mistake, walked into the bathroom. He didn't know what he was doing. Poor Gled. It was awful. He looked humped over and tortured, the way he'd looked when I first saw him on the phone at The Harvard Club, only this wasn't just about a lost nanny. Sort of staggering, he went out the proper door, bumping the frame, and I pulled the covers over my head. I heard the front door close, then slept.

When I woke up, Mom was sitting on the end of the bed, knitting. She was a wonderful knitter, but she only knit when she didn't feel good, when something had happened to one of her girls or a lover had left her. Then she sat and knit like another woman might drink or take opium. "She's Madame Defarging," I'd tell my friends. "Do not disturb or your name might get into the roster of stitches."

"I heard it all," she said.

"I'll be right back." When something bad happens with me, I don't knit; I go to the corner cupboard for the Scotch. I came back into the room with a Scotch over ice, no twist because of the time consideration. I remembered that pregnant women shouldn't drink and vowed this would be my last. I sat up in bed, bunching the pillows behind me, and took a sip, then I set it aside. It wasn't fair to the tiny struggling growth within me to submit it to such toxicity. Now that I'd cried and perked up a bit, I was able to think about the baby and begin to cherish it as, I stunningly realized, I would do for the rest of my life. This other being was coming to rule me. I began to understand Mom better, ruled by three as she had always been since I'd known her. I could never again think only of myself or put myself first. My life would heretofore turn around this human inside me who was currently the size of a freckle. I would become the hoverer, bustler, and plumper, maybe even the knitter. I would be Mom!

Mom still sat at the end of the bed. There were three mirrors in the room—we'd each had to have our own—and the afternoon light flashed from one to another.

"Is he Danny's little brother?" She gave me The Eyes, before which I could only speak the truth.

"I don't know."

I told her the whole story, how I hadn't taken my diaphragm when I left Alan. How, returning home, I'd made love to him by surprise. The next week I fell into the quarry and made love to Gled by surprise, also with no diaphragm.

"Why doesn't Gled know you're married?"

I explained about that too.

"You're hot-blooded, Effie, like me." She sounded proud of us both. "I was always an easy lay."

I didn't tell her I knew that and as a result had tried with all my might *not* to be like her. Anyhow, I was only easily laid when I was surprised.

She smiled. "Men have always been drawn to me, I'm happy to say." She put down her knitting, pleased with the thought. "Even now, old and fat as I am."

Old and fat and badly dressed, with no idea of hair coloring or makeup, she was, nevertheless, a woman one loved to be with—a woman of heart and wit and, I guess, passion.

It's very hard to think of one's mother as a sex object. For the most part, one doesn't want to. But I began to get a glimmer of the truth, which was that the beastly lawyers maybe hadn't taken advantage of her if she was so willing, if she was having so much fun. Still, just because you're an easy lay doesn't mean you don't get emotionally invested and hurt. I knew she'd been hurt a lot. I'd seen the knitting.

Right now I was thinking that I'd rather be the hurt one than the one who hurt Gled so bad he couldn't walk through a door.

"Are you going to let Alan assume the baby is his, Effie?"

"Even if it is his, Alan is not going to want to have a baby, I can promise you that."

"Surely he won't want you to lose it?"

"My feeling is that it isn't Gled's or Alan's, it's mine."

"That was certainly how I felt about you girls. Men come and go. They die, divorce, or leave. But your children are yours forever. Children are the treasure women are given in this life to offset all the suffering. Not that they don't cause suffering too." Taking up her knitting again, she gave me a glance that said I was a prime example. It wasn't exactly "You take the cake!"—but close.

"I don't want to hear Alan tell me to get an abortion. That would really be the end of us."

"Don't tell him until you're in the second trimester."

"But what if it isn't his? I feel like I've got to go off and have this baby on my own, Mom. I'll go to San Francisco, finish my thesis among all Benny's work, and come home triumphant with baby and done dissertation."

"You've got to give Alan a chance, Effie. We'll go down this weekend. Tell him you're pregnant and see what he says. It's only fair. Don't prejudge him. If his paternal instincts take over and he wants the child, then it's for you to decide whether or not to tell him about Gled."

I began to wonder again, for perhaps the fiftieth time, if that trip to the Vietnam Veterans Memorial to see my father's name had been all that important, since he probably wasn't my father. I'd never cared to know one way or the other, but now that I was having a baby of my own, maybe it was important to know the complete family history. There might be madness or diseases on my father's side. For that matter, come to think of it, maybe it was more important for my baby (and me) to know the identity of his father than my father.

I suppose there are blood tests, I thought dismally. Now there is the DNA test. Never before could a man know for sure. He could know he was not the father but not that he was. Could a man get a DNA test on a child without permission from the mother? If he found out he was the (unmarried) father, did that give him rights to the child, even if the woman was married to another? Or even if she wasn't? It wasn't fair. Men still shouldn't be able to know.

I disregarded the fact that I didn't know either.

"Mom, don't tell the girls about this, okay?"

"But they'll be so happy! By the way, I haven't told you how happy I am. A grandmother! My dearest wish come true."

"I thought your dearest wish come true was my marrying Alan."

"It was," she said comfortably, "but then I needed another dearest wish."

"I think your dearest wish should be to go to law school

now that your children are all grown up and self-supporting. You're only forty-six. You'll be done in three years and still have sixteen years to practice!"

"I'm happy as I am, sweetheart." She lifted the knitting and smiled. "A baby blanket," she said.

That night Edna and Ellie, wouldn't you know, accused me of being pregnant. "We've got our periods and you don't," they said. "Proof."

"Listen," I expostulated mildly, "we used to all get our periods together when I lived here with you, but I don't live here anymore."

We were all on my single bed—three adult women jammed into their childhood room. Lucky we were all so small.

"You've been here almost five days," they expostulated back—as if I could get onto their rhythm in five days. Hopeless! As if one's body could click on where it left off a year ago. I'd been living with Alan a year before we married, known him for two.

"It takes months to get on your roommate's cycle," I explained reasonably, "not four days." I talked calmly. A few years ago I would have screamed it, but I'd come to grips with their idiocy and could handle it, probably thanks to T'ai Chi.

Of course, in this case, idiotic though their thinking was, they were right.

"Your breasts are bigger too," said Ellie.

"That's from marriage in general. Massage."

"Really?"

"No, I'm kidding."

"Mom's knitting a baby blanket," said Edna. I began to think they were incredibly keen and I was the idiot. "It would be so mean of you not to tell us if it's true." Edna began to sob and Ellie took up the lament, sobbing along with her.

I felt like a rat. And a snake. And partly like a pheasant.

"Okay, I'm pregnant. But I haven't told Alan yet."

Sobs gave way to merriment and to talking all night. It was fun. My depression was over for now. At least until I told Alan about Danny's little brother.

Snake creeps down, slithers away, coils up, then uncoils, stops being a snake, and becomes a happily pregnant woman.

"Hello?"

"Hi, Danny."

"Hi, Dad."

"One more last goodbye, like the song says."

"Do you have to go?"

"Yes. Duty calls. But I'll be back in November and meanwhile I'll call you as often as I can. You're the big fourth-grader now. Study hard and help your mom around the house."

"Okay."

"I love you."

"Love you, Dad. Mom wants to say goodbye too."

"Hi, Gled. Just want to wish you well."

"Thanks, Lynn."

"I have to admit I'm curious. Danny said he thought you liked the *au pair* quite a lot."

"Yes, I did, but she's out of the picture. There's someone else in her life."

"Are you sure Janice didn't pay her to say so."

"Effie wouldn't take any crap from Janice."

"Then she's a better woman than I."

"Janice didn't end our marriage. You did."

"She was a big strain on it. Once she got her heir, she wanted her little brother for herself again."

"Do you want back in the marriage, Lynn?"

"Good God, no."

"Then why don't you drop the subject?"

"Fair enough. It's just that you're so clueless. I'm sure if you liked this Effie, you told Janice, and I'm sure she hightailed it up to the quarry and warned her off. Danny said she left suddenly."

"She and Janice had words. Effie told her to fuck off and Janice fired her, but her time was up anyway. It was something else that made her get out of my life. So let's drop that subject too. Goodbye. I'll be calling Danny whenever I'm in civilization."

"Goodbye, Gled. Take care."

"Hi, Janice. It's Gled."

"I can talk for two minutes."

"It will only take one. Just to tell you I'm off to Ecuador on a flying job. I'll be back for the holidays and I'll have Danny for Thanksgiving. Let's plan to have it here at the quarry."

"Fine with me. What about your little nanny?"

"I asked Effie to marry me again and she told me she's pregnant, not necessarily with my child. I have to say it killed me. A change of locale will do me good. A change of air to be airborne in."

"Be careful."

"I will. Bye."

"Hello?"

"Hello, Martha, this is Emma Crackalbee."

"Hello, Emma. What a surprise! Is Jane all right? Alan told me she'd gone home again."

"She's fine. She was feeling a little low. We're coming down to Lanesville for Labor Day weekend."

"How nice."

"Yes. Very nice. Martha . . ."

"Yes?"

"I'm being a busybody, but I want you to know that Effie is pregnant."

"Really? My goodness. Heavens!"

"Yes. We—me and the girls—are thrilled of course."

"Of course! Come to think of it, I feel rather thrilled myself. A little grandchild? How marvelous. Jane is full of surprises."

"She hasn't told Alan yet. She'll tell him when we come down, but, Martha, she is very afraid he will want her to abort the child. I thought maybe you could talk to him first. It's important that he be gentle with her."

"Alan is not a hard man. He is a very gentle person."

"Of course. But she thinks he won't want the child."

"I assure you he'll want the child. He probably didn't plan on one so soon, but he is infinitely flexible. He'll soon adjust to the idea and be in seventh heaven. It's too bad he started his novel—so hard to write with screaming babies and then there's his teaching too. I guess he'd hoped to give up his teaching to finish the novel, but now he'll need the money. Not that I can't help out financially, but I doubt he'll accept it. Well, I am just thinking aloud, dear. Leave everything to me."

"I know you have a strong influence on him."

"Nothing like yours on Jane. My God, she's run home to Mother twice in a month. It must be a record."

"I understand you and Alan talk on the phone two or three times a day and that he can hardly make a move without you."

"Nonsense."

"Well, I love to see children close to their mother."

"And to their grandmother too, I bet. I'll talk to Alan, dear. *Au revoir.*"

"Alan, it's your mother."

"I'm writing."

"It's no good to say you're writing and can't talk. If you're honestly writing, you simply don't pick up the phone to begin with."

"I must say it's hard having a mother who's such a fucking authority."

"I should write a book: *Writers I Have Known—and Been."*

"What's up?"

"Jane's pregnant. Her mother just called to tell me to prepare you. She's going to tell you this weekend. Alan?

"Alan . . . ?"

"Is Jane there?"

"No, Alan, she isn't. She's feeling so much better, she's gone shopping with the girls."

"Maternity clothes?"

"Alan, you don't sound very happy about this. Won't you wait until Effie tells you herself? Surely you're not going to try to discuss it on the phone."

"You mean like you did?"

"Okay, I was being a busybody, I know it, but . . ."

"Do you think this is the sort of news you want to hear from your mother-in-law by way of your mother? Or do you want to hear it from your wife?"

"You have no right to speak so harshly to me. I'm simply looking out for my daughter and my grandchild as best I can. Alan?"

{13} Embrace the Tiger to Return to the Mountain

You begin facing north, feet parallel, arms crossed, and you achieve the position called Embrace the Tiger to Return to the Mountain in one hip-opening step that is quite a balancing act and turns your body so that it faces southeast.

You aren't taking steps per se. You move from the *tan t'ien,* just below the abdomen, and the arms and legs follow suit. The *chi* (energy) is pooled in the *tan t'ien* and, if all goes well, makes a sanguinary spread to all parts of your body, which, being relaxed and open, allows for this circulatory splendor.

Which is why, at the end of the form, you are refreshed, alert, energized, and your body is all a-tingle. Not only is your circulation and metabolism up to snuff and your muscles exercised, but your internal organs have been massaged by the mystical movements first evolved by the Taoist saint Chang San-feng between the twelfth and thirteenth centuries.

So return to the seashore and embrace the tiger. While Emma, Edna, and Ellie were lugging porch pillows down to the rocks to sunbathe, Alan and I made love tigerishly. I'd resolved to do my best to cement the marriage and there's nothing like semen for adhesiveness, especially because, since my surprise lovemaking with Gled, I'd been rather denying Alan. And myself.

It was a good one. We vocalized. Alan went, *"Uw-uw-uw,"* and I went, *"Oh-oh-oh,"* and afterward we sprawled on the bed—sweaty, puffed, and happy. Now would be a good time to tell him about the little treasure coming our way. But, even feeling relaxed and replete as I did, I felt anxious too. Too bad. It should be such a joyful announcement, but I just didn't feel Alan would be overjoyed. No spinning around the room for him.

Although I was training myself not to think of Gled, I remembered his exhilarated twirl and his subsequent blind-man's-buff exit and it made it even harder to tell Alan. I should be content that one man responded happily and not feel I had to have a two-out-of-two response of unqualified joy, right? Except that this one was the husband. He was the one I needed to want the child that, I felt in my heart and womb, was his.

Another thing was that with Gled, the news just burst out along with my tears, whereas this was a calculated announcement. I like the bursting out approach better. It's natural and sincere.

I was definitely having qualms. I began to entertain the idea of not telling Alan, at least for a while, and the relief I suddenly experienced was like a shot of morphine. I felt so happy I fell asleep.

But it was only for a minute or two. Alan's voice roused me. "I thought you'd choose this moment to tell me the big news."

I looked at him, sincerely bewildered. "News?"

"About the baby," he said, rather grimly I thought.

"You know?"

"I know."

I sat up and cut to the chase. "Are you glad?"

"I'm not glad about hearing about it from my mother, who heard about it from your mother."

From the open window I heard screams and squeals signifying that Ellie and Edna were braving the freezing water. Good for them. Whenever they came to Lanesville, they took advantage of every minute of seashore life, unlike Alan's friends, who just ate and drank.

"But are you glad about the baby?" I asked Alan.

He frowned. I could tell he had to get the mother business out of the way first. He was a one-step-at-a-time man, he was wounded by the way he'd heard, and he needed to acquaint me with his reaction to the badly dispensed news.

"I'm sorry, Alan. Mom found out by mistake. I didn't know she'd called Martha. I honestly didn't. It was a horrible way for you to hear."

There. Now maybe he'd tell me his feelings about the child.

"I suppose Heedless and Needless know too. Before me."

"Only because, based on wrong information, they rightly guessed."

I felt interrogated, not a good feeling. This was supposed to be a joyful announcement, not a grim inquisition. "Alan, we're going to have a baby. What are your feelings? Are you happy?"

"Mother called. Everything important she has to say to me she always says by phone. Why can't she get in her car and come the hell over? It wasn't even like spreading good news. It was like a warning: 'The sky is falling.' There are things you don't want to hear by phone, like birth or death warnings, like your life is about to be totally wrecked. You want to hear it in person from your wife."

"Of course you do. That's why I've come down." *Wrecked?*

"But why did you go away when you learned that you were pregnant?"

"I was late with my period. I took a home test, so I didn't hear it in person either. It threw me. I had to get away"—under the covers—"and come to grips. Alan, do you want this baby?"

First I would find out if he wanted it and if he did, I would have to tell him about the Danny's-little-brother possibility, whereupon he would not want the baby—or me. But I would take that when it came, when I heard what he said in person. I guess this was a test. Another home test.

"It's a big decision," he said.

Murder always is, I wanted to say. Up until now I'd been completely proabortion and I still would be for others. For myself I wouldn't dream of it. I wanted this child with all my heart. I wanted lots of children. I was so surprised at myself. Previously the hardworking, overly disciplined intellectual, I now wanted nothing more than to be a barefoot, childbearing birdwatcher. I felt full of life, literally and figuratively. I was embracing the tiger.

"I want to have children with you, Jane. I just don't feel now is the time. We've only been married two months. I've finally begun my novel. I was thinking of teaching this fall and winter, then taking a year's sabbatical in the spring. With you and Mother whipping me on, I think I can finish the novel in a year. I know I sound selfish. But the baby is only a few weeks old and the procedure would not be traumatic. I'm only asking you to wait. Please. I don't think I'm being unreasonable."

He wasn't. He was being completely reasonable. I felt sad. I felt disappointed. But I did not feel the anger I'd expected to feel. I could see it from his side. He looked truly troubled. I felt sad, but mostly for him—for what he was doing to us and himself.

I walked to the window and watched my sisters flailing around in the water. Mom too. They were having a wonderful time. Farther out, two divers were going for lobster, an inflated rubber ring with a flag signaling their presence. Even farther out, a sailboat race was under way, the boats approaching the buoy on a beat, then shooting into the wind to reach it (lingo I'd learned from Alan). What a day! All the more glorious for not being summer, only looking like summer in September.

"I understand," I said to Alan. I did.

"Thank God!" He came over and embraced me. "I've been so afraid you wouldn't understand. The truth is: I never know what you're going to do, how you're going to react to things. You're full of surprises. You definitely keep me on my toes." He laughed.

I smiled. I hugged him back slightly, gently, as if he were frail. He was frail.

"I think I'll go swimming," I said. I grabbed a towel from the bathroom and, stark naked, went downstairs, out the door, across the porch, the green, over the rocks, and down to the water's edge. After all, why not be naked? It was all family here. The divers were underwater. Gled and Danny did it all the time at their house. Why not me at my house? The three E's, toweling themselves, shrieked to see me and fell about laughing. I jumped into the water and surfaced. "Effie," they screamed, "you can't swim!" They all dove in to save me.

"I can float!" I assured them, sputtering as I surfaced. "Danny taught me."

They clustered around me, all three of them treading water while I floated on my back. "Did you tell Alan? What did he say?"

"He wants to wait. He doesn't want this baby." They all fell silent. No one said anything. One by one they swam back to the rocks and clambered out, rewrapping themselves in towels. I floated. My arms and legs were spread. My hair fanned out around my head. I looked at the sky. Inside me, my minuscule baby was floating too. Nothing to look at for her. Probably no eyes yet with which to look. But she was there, and there she would remain until she was ready to come out and see the wondrous blue bell of heaven for herself. Together we would embrace the tiger.

Dear Danny:

I have discovered another bird that doesn't walk. It is called Magnificent Frigatebird and like the hummingbird, it is a superaerialist, but not because it beats its wings so fast—because it doesn't beat its wings at all! The wings are long and narrow, seven and a half feet from tip to tip, and it can fly for days without a wing stroke! It even eats on the wing, seizing food from the surface of the water or swiping fish from other seabirds when they arise from the water with their catch. It doesn't walk or swim and rarely roosts. It's an air walker, a hang glider. It's an air rider and raider.

How's the magnificent skateboarder? Any new moves? I miss you here on the faraway other coast.

Love always,
Effie

Dear Effie:

I miss you too. School's boring, but I have a new friend, John, I can skateboard with. He's cool. Dad's coming home for Thanksgiving and we'll go to the quarry, which is good, except Janice will be there.

Love,
Danny

P.S. Thanks for telling me about the Magnificent Frigatebird.

{14} Tiger Attack

How I treasured that little note from Danny, read it again and again. I was so lonely. It was great being in a new city by myself, feeling more free and independent than I ever had, but the downside was loneliness. I missed everybody so much. Mom was great about calling and I talked to Alan too but in a perfunctory way because he assumed I'd gone to San Francisco for an abortion and to do thesis research and it's hard to have any sort of conversation with someone who is so deluded. But I didn't want to straighten him out because I no longer felt my life was his business. At the same time, I didn't want to get a divorce until the baby was born. I guess I had an old-fashioned streak and wanted her to be legitimate. I left Lanesville that day, simply telling Alan that I wanted to be on my own for a while and was going to the other coast and that I would inform Harvard not to expect me to be around.

A day later I was in San Francisco, staying with two friends from college and looking for a room of my own.

These friends were embarked on such a different life—parties, dates, jobs, decorating their apartment—that I couldn't talk with them either. I let them too think I was here doing research, that I was a well-married woman with an intellectual goal. Of course, I would try to do research on Benny. I couldn't just sit in a room for eight months, doing nothing.

School's boring . . .

I imagined Danny, big-eyed and tousle-haired, sitting at his desk, looking out the window, dreaming of skateboard exploits, of flying as his father flew—only, for Danny, for now, just a foot or two off the ground, which was enough for him because it wasn't how high, how far, or how fast, it was just being there. In the air. For Danny's moment in the air, time expanded. He could soar, do twists, turns, and flips before letting his wheels reconnect with the ground. Just as Gled, with his parachuting partners, could form patterns in the air as if he weren't plummeting ninety miles per hour toward earth at the same time, until, almost in the spirit of an afterthought, he would open the chute and float safely to touch the ground that was no longer rushing toward him.

For me, it was hard to imagine wanting to defy the natural human condition like that. With my T'ai Chi, I tried to be more and more grounded, to root into the earth until I was untopple-able. Maybe I was crane spreading wings, but I wasn't anywhere near flying or wanting to. I wanted to be grounded but with wings spread, ready to embrace tiger.

. . . I have a new friend, John, I can skateboard with. He's cool.

That was good. Danny was so advanced for his age in the skateboard discipline that he was usually a lone skater. Now he had a cool pal. A friend is everything. Especially with his dad away.

Dad's coming home for Thanksgiving and we'll go to the quarry . . .

I had a huge longing to go to the quarry too and be with them. I felt so much that Danny was my son.

. . . except Janice will be there.

Still, I'd go if I could, even with Janice there, if it meant seeing Danny. And Gled.

Yes, I thought a lot about Gled, his strong brave body and good loving-overboard heart.

Where would *I* be for Thanksgiving?

"Hello, Emma, dear. This is Martha."

"What a surprise."

"I've called for two reasons. First, how is Jane doing in San Francisco? I get reports from Alan, but they are so unsatisfactory. You know how men are."

"Not really. But I suppose you mean lacking in detail."

"Yes."

"Well, Effie is living in a boardinghouse in a not-great location but at least not a dangerous one. She has a hot plate in her room and a bathroom down the hall. Two of her friends from college are in the city and she sees them, so that's good. She's gathering a lot of material for her thesis. Bufano's sculptures are all around the Bay Area. There are some people alive, still, who knew Bufano. She has even met his son, who presides over the Bufano Society for the Arts, which is amazing, considering Bufano denied he was his child and cast off his mother in her pregnancy. It would sort of be like Alan and Effie's child presiding over Alan's house as a historical landmark in the years to come—if he became a great writer, that is, and if their child had been allowed to live."

"That's a very unkind cut, Emma. You know very well that Alan and Jane agreed together that it was not a propitious time to have this child but that they would have another in due course."

"That's what Alan *told* Effie when she asked him if he wanted the child."

"He was very upset by the way he heard, so it was partly you and me who queered the deal. Mostly you, Emma."

"When I called to ask you to tenderly prepare Alan, I didn't mean for you to call him up and bluntly *warn* him."

"Well, it's water over the dam now. The point is: We're still family and the second reason I called is to invite you and the girls down for Thanksgiving. I hope Jane will be home too, but in any case we'd love to have you. There will be about fifteen of us. It's traditional to gather strays for the occasion."

"It's very thoughtful of you to count us among your strays, but . . ."

"Really, Emma, you're being very trying today. I said you were *family.* The others are the strays."

"Anyhow, we always go to my dead husband's family on Thanksgiving. I'm sorry we can't join you and Alan and the strays, but thank you for thinking of us. Let's stay in touch. *O reservoir.*"

"What?"

"Alan, it's Martha. Emma and the girls aren't coming. They go to her husband's family. She seems quite indignant about the baby. She is out a grandchild and feeling wronged by us all. I must say she can express herself too. She has a nice ironic edge when she wants to. I used to think she was such a dullard. Then, at the end of the conversation, she said, *'O reservoir.'* Why are you laughing?"

"I'm just wishing I'd thought of it. It's from E. F. Benson. The Lucia series. Lucia always said that in parting."

"So she reads too."

"You're such a snob."

"Emma says Jane is in a boardinghouse. Are you sending her money?"

"She said not to. She said she wanted to use the money she earned this summer."

"I think you should be helping her, Alan."

"Don't meddle."

"Please give me her address."

"I'll fax it over to you. Bye, Mom."

"A tout à l'heure."

"Janice, darling, this is Martha. I hear you're coming to Lanesville for Thanksgiving. Since we'll be there too, I want to urge you to join us for turkey."

"No thanks, Martha. We'll get together at some point, but dinner will be with my brother and nephew, the old couple who care for the house, and some close friends of Gled. I always spend the holidays with Gled. We've never been apart for them. Thanks, though. How's the book coming?"

"Swimmingly."

"There's someone on the other line."

"Goodbye, then."

"Happy Thanksgiving, Effie, sweetheart. Did you have a nice day?"

"Very nice. I spent it with my friends in their Pacific Heights apartment. It was a real party. But now I'm happy to be back in my burrow. I get so tired these days."

"That's how it was with me when I was carrying you girls. I'd drop off at the oddest times."

"I met a birder. He's going to take me to Bolinas, where he lives in a house that has the second-biggest yard list in North America. That means from the yard, actually a deck, he can see more bird species than can be seen from any other house. He lives on the Bolinas lagoon, so it's mainly seabirds, including the Great Blue Heron and the American Egret. I'm so excited."

"That's great. Well, get some sleep and I'll call you again in a few days. I love you."

"I love you, Mom."

"This is Lynn speaking. Happy Thanksgiving!"

"Lynn, it's Gled."

"Gled? Your voice. Why do you sound like that? Something's happened to Danny, hasn't it? Oh God, No, Gled, no!"

"Yes. Something has happened. I'm coming to get you."

"Alan, it's Mom. I tried to call you all last night. Where were you?"

"I decided to stay in Lanesville. Slept in front of the fire."

"Alan, listen, before I drove to the city, I stopped in the village and there had been a tragic accident."

"Yes, I heard. I don't want to talk about it, if you don't mind."

"But, Alan . . ."

"Later. Bye."

"Alan, you can't cut me off like that. I have to find out what you know. The child is the nephew of my agent, Janice, and before I call her, I have to know if he lived or died."

"The village doesn't know. Some say he was dead. Some say his face wasn't covered when they put him in the ambulance."

"How can a whole village not know? I gather it was a skateboarding accident, but was there a car involved too?"

"I'm sorry, that's all I know."

"Well, I better call Janice. These things are so difficult. Oh dear. Goodbye."

"Janice, it's Martha. I heard about your nephew. I just want to say how terribly sorry I am. My deepest sympathy, dear. It's a tragedy."

"Thank you, Martha. I really can't talk . . ."

"I understand. Please call on me if I can do anything . . ."

"Wait. I do want to talk. I need to. It's so terrible to realize there's no one to go to at such a time. I feel so alone. I was always closest to Gled, but he's too devastated to say a word."

"Oh dear . . ."

"You see, Danny asked me if he could go skateboarding and I said no. He said his nanny, the *au pair* we had last summer, that Effie, always used to let him skate on High Street. Well, that got me mad and we had a big fight about it. He wanted to ask his Dad, but I wouldn't let him disturb him. He'd only just got in from Central America. Then all was quiet and I got suspicious. When I couldn't find Danny anywhere, I realized he must have sneaked off with his skateboard. I was furious. I got in the car and went after him. So it was I who found him. It was I who had to tell Gled."

"It's tragic. But was he? Is he . . . ?"

"Here come Gled and Lynn now. I've got to go."

"Alan, dear, it's your mother. I'm sorry to disturb you, but you should know . . . that accident in Lanesville . . . it was the little boy Jane was nanny for. She went by the name Effie there."

"Yes, it was Danny."

"Alan, why didn't you tell me?"

"I didn't know when we last talked."

"Will you tell Jane? Don't you think she should know?"

"No, I can't. It's like . . . first I tell her to kill our child and now this kid she really loved might be dead."

"But . . ."

"I know it's crazy, but now I feel like a murderer. I didn't before when it was our child. Now I do. Please don't talk to me anymore about it. Leave me alone for a while. I feel crazy."

"But is he dead? I still don't know. I talked to Janice, but I could hardly outright ask her and she never said one way or the other."

"Then call the fucking hospital."

"Good grief!"

"Emma, it's Martha."

"Hello, Martha. How was your Thanksgiving?"

"It ended tragically. You know the little boy Jane took care of last summer? He had a skateboarding accident. The whole village is grieving. Apparently his father, whom I've never met, is much loved. The boy was too."

"Is he dead?"

"He's hovering. I called the hospital. He's in a coma."

"Danny. His name is Danny."

"Oh dear. Are you crying?"

". . ."

"I thought maybe Jane should know. She might want to come back."

"I . . . I just don't think I should tell her. Not now. It would be too much for her."

"What do you mean, 'Not now'?"

"It would break her heart. I'll . . . I'll talk to you later. Thanks for calling to tell me about Danny, Martha. I really appreciate it."

"Alan, it's Martha. I'm sorry to be hounding you, but I just have to talk to you again. This whole thing is affecting me. I feel so . . . sort of scared. Now they're saying it was a hit-and-run. The thing is: I remember you drove out that morning. You often take that High Street way to the village, I don't know why, and there's your terrible driving, and then saying you felt like a murderer. Well, I just need terribly to be reassured that you weren't involved. Or, if you were, talk to me about it. Please. I feel so frightened for you."

"I was not involved."

"Thank God. Thank God! I love you, darling. It's times like this that one realizes . . . Well, if I were ever to lose you . . ."

"Then why do you accuse me?"

"I wasn't accusing . . ."

"You accused me. My own mother."

"I'm sorry if it sounded like that. Please forgive me."

"Forget it. I'm sorry. I feel so angry with everyone. I wish . . . I wish Jane were here. I wish things . . . I . . . had been different."

"Call her. Do. Tell her you want her to come home."

"I can't. Especially now I can't."

{15} Grasp the Sparrow's Tail

Grasp the Sparrow's Tail is an oft-repeated posture in the T'ai Chi form, a defense posture, warding off with your right or left hand, your weight distributed 70 percent on the front foot, 30 percent on the back. With the completion of any T'ai Chi move, weight is almost always 70–30, because equal weight on each foot is a dangerous, unprepared way to stand. T'ai Chi is first and foremost a martial art and every move when speeded up is either a strike or a repulse.

By now my feet and legs were fast disappearing from sight behind my ever-expanding belly, so I simply had to trust that my extremities knew what they were doing.

I was spending my pregnancy in a warding-off posture, not forming any alliances or relationships except with the infant growing within. At the same time, I was trying to grasp not just the sparrow's tail but the entire breathtaking kingdom of birds. I was deeply absorbed and spending most of my time with Peter and Keith, two birders (one of whom I'd met on Thanksgiving) who were generous at imparting their knowledge and lending me books (some of which they'd written), as well as letting me stay at the house of the famous yard list. They were caretakers of the house and I became a subcaretaker (i.e., house cleaner, a lower-than-ever job I didn't tell my sisters about).

Keith was big, bluff, full of life and the joy of birds. He looked like a wrestler but was a bird artist of the most delicate strokes, a self-educated ornithologist. Peter, mild and ethereal, was a naturalist. Both men were highly respected in the field. They had girlfriends, so I didn't need to ward off. They liked being friends and mentors. They liked having the freedom to go off on expeditions and leave the house in my hands.

I was at the other end of the continent in another shore house by another ocean. It was on a lagoon within sight of the coastal hills that nightly absorbed the sunset light in a way so subtle and mysterious and beautiful that it seemed like something more than a sunset was going on. Here I did my T'ai Chi morning and evening on the deck which was set over the tideswept water rushing either into or out of the lagoon. Here the air, sand, and sea were awash with birds: gulls, terns, egrets, herons, shearwaters, sanderlings, vultures, hawks, hummingbirds, swallows, sparrows, to name but a tiny portion of the yard list. None of them was ever alarmed by the meditative T'ai Chi action that was like the movement of air or water itself, the action of reflections and shadows.

Across the lagoon from the house was the Audubon Canyon Ranch, where one could observe through fixed binoculars the Great Blue Herons and Great Egrets, the largest of the coastal birds, nesting in the redwood trees, see them wing from the tall trees to the lagoon to search for small fish and other marine organisms, then fly back to the canyon to resume their duties in the colossal stick nests that, next to a hummingbird's nest, looked as though they were made of logs.

I had two nests: the room in the city and the room on the lagoon. I had begun my San Francisco stay seeking out Benny's sculptures, prepared to put the spotlight of my brain on each and every one, but the art left me cold and the search soon became desultory, and now, steeped in bird lore, I no longer even pretended to myself that I was working on my thesis.

Although magnificently located on a mesa by the sea, the town of Bolinas itself was a scruffy one. It boasted a population of poets and birders but looked to me full of people of indeterminate age, part hippie, part redneck, wholly in need of showers, driving old pickups accompanied by flea-bitten dogs. I don't know what fantasy they were living in or what ostensible decade. Here the ward-off posture suited me fine.

The Bolinas Border Patrol tore down any signs to the town that the California Highway Patrol put up, so as to maintain its integrity as a town off the beaten track, closed to tourists. If anyone tried to put in a little shop that might attract a tourist or two, he got hate mail from the BBP. You practically got hate mail if you painted your house or wore a new dress. Even though I wore clean clothes and washed my hair, I was tolerated because I was pregnant and abandoned.

My lagoon room was like a ship's cabin, containing a single bed, a table, and a closet. It was all I wanted. I was considering not returning to the East Coast—if it weren't for Mom. I missed her a lot and it would be such a shame to separate her from her grandchild. She was going to come out here for the delivery. Maybe I could persuade her to stay—if she could ever divorce the law firm. The girls could move out too. Why not? They were free as birds. Life here would be so much richer for them. They were already Californians at heart.

Probably, on some level, Alan knew I wasn't coming back. Our phone conversations were becoming less frequent and extremely withholding. It was a contest who could say the least about their life and still not outright lie. Up until Thanksgiving, he had been his same old loving, interfering self, then he turned cold and morose. I figure he maybe had learned about my keeping the baby, but I wasn't going to ask. My not asking what was wrong was the beginning of our ever-increasing withholdingness. Previously we had always talked things out. But what was there for me to say? The fact was: I was having a baby he'd asked me not to have. Where do you go from there? West. As far west as you can go continentally and then, amazingly, one step farther.

To the Farallon Islands. In mid-March, seven and a half-months pregnant, I was invited by Peter, who was impressed by my assiduous study, to spend a couple of weeks at an isolated sanctuary, a place banned to the public: the Farallon Islands, twenty-seven miles west of the Golden Gate, the last bit of America before Hawaii, a rookery for birds and sea elephants.

Peter went on ahead and I left a few days later. It took two hours by fishing boat, which was carrying supplies to the island. It was a clear day and the craggy, jagged outline ahead gradually resolved into individual islands, some little more than large rocks, the two biggest being no more than one hundred and twenty acres or three-fourths of a mile by half a mile.

When I arrived, there appeared to be no harbor per se, no pier, no berth for the boat. We eased into a small inlet where waves were smashing against rocks on all sides. "Go to the bow," directed the captain. Put this on!" He handed me a life jacket. "Quick." Obediently, I did what he said. The boat heaved up and down. I grasped the railing. What now? I was mesmerized by the swirling foam we rode on and drenched by the spray the waves tossed back from the rocky shore. Above, on the cliff, was a crane (not the wing-spreading kind) and its boom was lowering a cargo net containing a rubber tire to the bow of the fishing boat. "Step onto the tire and hold onto the net with all your might!" shouted the captain.

I thought if I was going to be hoisted up to the island by this method, which I hoped wasn't true, I should be *in* the net, not holding on to the outside of it, but there was no time to think, only to obey. I stepped onto the tire, grasped the net, and was soon being hoisted aloft—up, up, above the wave-tossed boat—then swung over to the land and lowered onto the guano-encrusted stones.

An alien landscape greeted my eyes—a seeming moonscape because of the shit-whitened ground. No trees. No plants that you'd notice. Two forlorn white wooden houses turned algae-green. Birds. It was beautiful.

One house belonged to the Coast Guard and was used by the lighthouse keepers; the other belonged to the Point Reyes Bird Observatory, a branch of the one in Bolinas. Here I was installed in the Jane Fonda suite, the female dorm, so named because of a portrait of Barbarella that had hung there until some British feminist birders took it down.

There did turn out to be trees on the island, the "Farallon National Forest," consisting of two Monterey cypress trees and one Monterey pine, and there were plants too, growing out of the guano-enriched rock, Farallon weeds that would burst into golden bloom while I was there. As for the birds, there were a quarter of a million of them.

I was honored to be allowed into this wildlife fraternity. I spent the weeks behind wooden blinds, from which I observed the birds and the preposterous sea elephants. I was developing an eye. I was beginning to learn how to see color and shape within the blur of motion. One feather could make all the difference to the veracity of what I thought I saw. Conversely, the sea elephants hardly moved at all. Towering heaps of blubber, the pregnant females snoozed in the sun—when it wasn't raining, which was most of the time. They snoozed in the rain and the shrieking winter winds and in the spray of the thirty-foot waves that rammed the island like runaway trucks. I, lying in a similar position, on my side and similarly blubbery because of my big belly, also did my share of snoozing. The sometimes-bellowing, sometimes-bloody-battling bulls were fifteen to eighteen feet long and up to six thousand pounds. Thirty-five years ago these creatures were almost extinct. One of nature's comeback stories!

It's wonderful how, once we stop killing creatures, they'll stage a comeback. That's all it takes.

I'd come far, geographically and emotionally. On a dot in the vast forever I nested with sea elephants to the tune of crashing waves. I could be in Patagonia. I was not a Harvard intellectual. I was a pregnant woman, full of life, who lay down on hard wet ground to wait, watch, and learn.

It was all mystifying. How had my life taken such a turn? Had it really begun in the community garden with the Cardinal? At night, in the stark wooden building, eating horrible dinners that we took turns cooking, I listened to the scientists and naturalists and understood very little. I was out of my element, a rank beginner, which was a new experience. Always, anywhere, I could hold my own or at least fake it. Not here. Mostly I listened to the rhythms of their vitality and enthusiasm, their *chi.* I wallowed in the *chi* of these men and women who were so close to nature, so in love with it, these stewards of our environment, guardians of our wildness. I wasn't one of them, not yet. For now I was a lone cleaning lady and young-carrier.

{16} Not Grasping

It was early April before I got back to my room in the city, where I hadn't been for over a month. Someone had broken in and was inhabiting it. As I stood at the door, I was scared because it was almost a minute before I recognized that the man lying asleep on my bed was Gled.

He was so gaunt. Gone was the beefy splendor of his form. The springy curls on his head no longer sprang. His eyes, when they opened and gazed upon me, were dull and lifeless, reminding me how they always so crazily had lit up to see me or Danny, as if every vision of us was a gift, a marvel, a blessing. Talk about *chi.* Now that I beheld Gled so lifeless, I recognized him as a man of blazing energy—the wild man that Danny had spoken of so proudly. I had somehow always averted my eyes from Gled. My eyes were always for Danny or a book or a bird. He's dying, I thought with a chill to my heart. He has some terrible disease.

"Danny's gone," he said.

"No." I sat down next to him on the bed and he sat up beside me.

"He was skateboarding. A car hit him. It was a hit-and-run. There's no more Danny."

I couldn't grasp what he was saying. There was a ringing in my ears. "What?"

He repeated the intolerable words.

"When?"

"Thanksgiving." The words fell dully from his mouth, like stones, like boulders. I seemed to see the stones of words gathering at my feet. "I'd just gotten home from twenty hours in the air and was resting."

"You never rest," I said stupidly, but it was true. Gled would only lie down at night to sleep and then only for a few hours. How could he have rested then at that crucial hour?

The stones kept tumbling from the gap of his mouth. "Danny and Janice had a fight. She told him he couldn't skateboard and he couldn't wake me up to ask. He could have. Of course he could have awakened me. Why didn't he? Better to have disobeyed her in that than in the other. But what would I have said? Probably yes. Maybe I would have gone with him, but I might have said, 'Sure, son, go ahead.' Maybe he knew that. He went. He was a little scared of Janice and her wrath, but he still went. He thought it would still be worth it, High Street being prime skateboarding terrain."

"Oh, Danny," I keened. "Danny."

"When Janice realized he'd disappeared, she went after him in the car. She found him, called me from her car phone, called the ambulance."

I'd gone so far into myself that his words seemed to come from another room. "Danny," I moaned.

"Can you imagine someone crashing into a little boy, then driving away, leaving him there?"

I tried to attend. I wanted to know everything, but his stones of words had turned to drifting sand, to dust, barely discernable. "Did anyone see?" I asked.

"No. Everyone was either eating Thanksgiving dinner or away from their homes, dining with relatives. No one was around at all. I've gone up and down that block asking. I've gone around the whole village again and again. In any case, someone would have come forward if they'd seen anything. Danny's gone, Effie. He's gone. And I feel so alone. I just want to be with you. Will you marry me now? Please. Will you let me be a father to your baby?"

"Yes. Yes, of course."

"Thank you. I know I'm a wreck of a man to marry. But I'll come around. We'll be happy, Effie. Danny would be so glad. It's only recently I found out you were here all alone and going to have the baby."

"Mom?"

"Yes. But don't be angry with her. She held out for a long time. I practically had to tie her to a chair and torture the information out of her."

"Oh, Danny!" I cried. "Danny!" Gled put his arms around me and let me cry. He had no tears left after four months of crying.

"Danny's not really gone," he reassured me. "You have to understand."

"I do understand. He'll always be with us in our hearts. Always. Every day, every hour."

"But, really, Effie, he's not dead. He's not. He's only away."

We were married in the futuristic Frank Lloyd Wright Civic Center in San Rafael, California. When we got our license, they asked for any divorce dates and where and when we were born and the names of any children, but they didn't ask if I was already married. It was so simple. We did the paperwork, paid our money, got a witness, and a woman said some words over us in the garden in front of the fountain, the gold Wrightian spire soaring behind us above the aqua-colored domed roof. The fountain splashed, birds sang, the sky was Giotto blue, and the words were nice.

My wedding to Alan had been veil and gown to the ground (antique ones that had been Martha's mother's) at the Leslie Linsey Memorial Chapel on Boston's toney Arlington Street, stained glass galore, followed by a reception at the Tennis and Raquet Club. There were one hundred and fifty people, twenty of whom were my family and friends, the rest Alan and Martha's.

This wedding was much nicer, but we were both so grief-stricken that it seemed to make no impression. I didn't feel like a bride. Least of all did I feel like a bigamist. I was on another coast, in another world, three thousand miles away. Alan had relinquished us (me and the child.) That marriage was meaningless. So too was this one. It was not a marriage, it was a lifesaving procedure, no different from breathing air into Gled's lungs, as he had done to me the night of stepping backward into the quarry. He had saved my life and now I was saving his. It was the least I could do.

We made love that night, Gled entering my vagina from behind so as to avoid the cumbrous tummy. No putting me on his penis and twirling me around this time. He was gentle and careful. He held my breasts like chalices and buried his face in my hair and stroked my birth passage with his penis as if paving the way for the coming child. I was surprised how aroused I became, as I'd seen this as only part of my mission of mercy, something not exactly to suffer or even tolerate but to, well, comply with, submit good-naturedly to. But no. I went into an orgasmic frenzy, a transcendent period of what must actually have been sexual ecstasy, calling upon him urgently, exhorting him not to stop, to keep going on pain of death, and he did, he kept going heroically until I was a quivering organism and had lost five pounds of perspiration and was begging him to please, please have his orgasm and be done with it on pain of my death, and he came in a long, quivering, agonized way, as if the semen were being drawn from him against his will, as if it were from a cache of unshed tears locked up in an unexpected place that he'd been saving for one last round of grief.

And then, afterward, while I was drinking a pint of water and rinsing myself off down the hall in the shower where I tried to replace some water through my pores as well as my throat and hydrate through the bottom of my feet as I stood, there was a phone call, also down the hall, and someone called out, "Is there a Gled here?" and I imagined him dragging himself to the phone, knuckles to the floor, maybe even on hands and knees. When, berobed and betoweled, I stepped out of the bathroom, he was just replacing the receiver. He crushed me in his arms and said, "Danny's out of his coma."

Talk about a man misrepresenting himself when he marries! Alan's phantom novel was nothing compared to this phantom death. I was furious. I blew up. From sexual ecstasy to temper tantrum in twenty minutes, weight distributed 70–30.

{17} Push Hands

"Use four ounces to deflect a thousand pounds."

The martial aspect of T'ai Chi is called Push Hands. Using the ward-off, roll-back, press, pushes, and pulls in the form, and above all maintaining calm and balance, one defends or—if necessary—attacks. This old Chinese pugilistic art is also called metaphysical boxing. Toward the end of the Sung Dynasty (960–1278), the Taoist Chang San-feng first applied the philosophy of Lao-tze to boxing, substituting pliability and yielding for muscular power and bravery, substituting energy for force, standing like a mountain but being light as a feather.

Relaxation is the releasing of tension and the loosening of all muscles but not the giving away of energy. Calmness is serenity, composure—the relaxation of the spirit muscle as it were. Calmness is distilled courage—a courage willing to yield, willing to suffer losses (momentarily).

There is a picture of Cheng Man-ch'ing pushing a man up in the air with one hand while his other hand is hanging by his side in the softest, loosest way imaginable, as if his were the hand and arm of a raggedy doll. His face is without any expression at all. Maybe there is the merest smile because he is having fun.

"It is said, if others don't move, I don't move. If others move slightly, I move first" (Wu Yu-hsiang, 1812–1880).

The T'ai Chi master senses his attacker's move before it happens, reading the message his opponent is sending from his brain to his own muscles and nerves.

That is why, when you have mastered the secrets of T'ai Chi and a vicious blow is directed your way, even coming from behind you, you receive no blow because you suddenly vanish (step aside) and leave the blow-deliverer unbalanced with egg on his face.

Weight 70–30, I stepped out of Gled's arms, then I rolled back with my weight 100 percent on my left leg. I put my left palm on my right forearm, shifted my entire weight to my right leg, and, with the momentum of my lower torso (the *tan t'ien),* pressed my hand forward against Gled's chest. In this way, I unearthed him, which is to say he rose slightly into the air, lost his balance, and began rapidly backpedaling down the hall until he slammed into the wall at the end and crumpled to the floor.

Not having done any Push Hands practice since June, I was surprised and pleased. I was so pleased I forgot I was mad.

I walked down the hall to Gled, who said, "Where am I? What happened? How did you do that?"

He was putting it on a bit, pretending to be more groggy than he was, which made him lovable to me.

"It's called Push Hands. It's T'ai Chi, of course."

"You mean that pretty little dance you do each morning and evening ends in this? Shouldn't your hands be registered as lethal weapons? No? What about your Push? That should be registered for sure. You should have a License to Push."

I laughed and stretched out a hand to help him to his feet.

He smiled up at me. " 'World-Famous Aviator Demolished

by Pregnant Twerp.' Not fair, though. First you beat the stuffing out of me sexually."

"Come into the room. We've got to talk about Danny. You said he was dead."

"In a minute. My turn for the bathroom."

I straightened the bed and hung up our clothes. I put a pot of water on the hot plate to make coffee. I untoweled and brushed my hair. There was one window in the room and I drew back the cotton curtains I'd made for it so that I could see the lights and the stars. We were still in the city room where I'd found Gled yesterday. It would have been nice to wedding-night in Bolinas, but I wasn't sure the cleaning lady was allowed to do that sort of thing. Anyhow, the single bed there would have been impossible. My room at this cheap but clean boardinghouse had a double bed, a desk and bookshelves, two straight-back chairs, an armchair, and a fairly large closet. It was not an impossible space for two people who liked each other. Gled had suggested going to a fancy hotel, but it didn't seem appropriate to the funereal marriage. At least this was cozy.

"I didn't say Danny was dead. I never said that. I said he was gone. And he was gone." Gled, dressed in blue jeans with a towel around his neck, rummaged in his bag for a clean T-shirt. His hair was wet and slicked straight back, giving him a European look. His eyes were large and dark in his thinned-down face. His tiger teeth seemed too big for his lips to cover. He sat down in the armchair and I passed him his coffee. "I sat with him every day in the hospital. But it wasn't Danny. It was just a vacant body. Danny was gone. Finally I couldn't stand to go and see him not be there. So I came to find you." He blew on the coffee and sipped. "To make it more horrible, Lynn blamed me. She said I was irresponsible. When Danny was four years old, I took him on a bike ride. He rode on the back fender and held on to my waist. He had a helmet, thank God, and thank God he was in back of me, so when we crashed, I took the brunt of it and he only broke a leg and a few ribs. But Lynn never trusted me with Danny after that. She was always worried that something would happen. Especially at the quarry. She drove me nuts with her worries. And Danny too. But he was the carefullest little boy. You know that. He never tried to do anything he knew to be beyond his powers. He knew not to take chances, to scope things out. I taught him that. Lynn never understood that if I did dangerous things, I only did them because I knew exactly what I was doing, because I was trained and practiced and disciplined. A kid doesn't learn to be careful from being frightened and warned. He learns by being taught to know exactly what he's doing."

Gled drew a deep breath.

"I understand. But stop talking about Danny in the past tense. It's unforgivable that you told me he was gone, that you thought he was gone and that you still think so. He's alive and he's out of his coma. Rejoice!"

"Lynn says he doesn't know her. He doesn't remember anything," Gled said gloomily.

"Of course he doesn't. That's how comas are. His memory will come back gradually."

"What if it doesn't?"

"Okay, worst case. Suppose it doesn't. He'll still be alive. He'll make new memories."

"But he won't be Danny. He'll be someone else. He won't know me. He won't remember all the wonderful times. I'll be a stranger. Maybe he won't love me or even like me."

Even with Danny not dead and not comatose, Gled's sorrow seemed inconsolable. There was nothing I could say, but that didn't keep me from trying.

"Of course he'll love you. And he will be Danny. The essence of Danny won't be lost. You'll see."

"Lynn isn't going to let him stay with me anymore. She's

going to sue for sole custody on the basis of what happened. He won't have the chance to get to know me."

"She's just saying that. She's just speaking from the fear and the strain. Anyhow, she wouldn't win. Especially now that you're married. Did you tell her you're married?"

"Yes. And she said it was hateful of me, that I was just trying to replace Danny because I thought he was going to die."

"God!"

"You know I loved you and asked you to marry me before Danny's accident. But it's true too that I thought Danny was virtually dead and that with you I could have his little brother. I'm a selfish person."

"Who isn't?"

"You're not. You married me out of the goodness of your heart, but I believe and hope that you'll come to love me as I love you."

"I married you to piss Janice off."

"No, you didn't."

"No, I didn't. But that's a bonus."

"I hope you'll come to love Janice too."

"In your dreams."

"Let's go to bed, but please, please, please don't ask me to fuck you again."

An hour later Gled was snoozing away, but I was reading about bird behavior when there was a light tap at the door and the girl next door said, "Phone for you, Effie."

Speak of the devil, it was Janice. I surmised she was looking for Gled and was going to tell her to hold on when she began talking hard and fast. "Effie, I only just learned that you'd gone to San Francisco to have your baby. Gled told me last fall that you were pregnant, maybe with his child. Neither of us knew that you were going to keep it. I figure the reason you've gone so far away to have it is that you want it kept a secret and that you're going to put it up for adoption. Effie, I want to adopt that baby."

My mouth fell open. I was speechless, for one of the few times in my life.

"I'll pay you, Effie. A lot. You can name your price."

My mouth closed, but my brain was reeling.

"It's for Gled," Janice went on. "You've heard about Danny . . . ?"

Thank God I didn't hear about Danny this way. I was so mad I tried to invoke a little Push Hands action via satellite. I poured a bunch of *chi* into the mouthpiece, then covered it with my hand so it wouldn't escape back into the hallway.

"Are you there?" Janice asked.

"Janice, listen to me. Danny's alive. And he's out of his coma. Everything is going to be all right." I don't know why I was responding so nicely. I guess because I knew she was doing this for love of Gled. Family love is something I understood and admired, even if hers was twisted.

"I know that. But even if Danny's going to be half all right, Gled has still as good as lost him because Lynn's being such a bitch. Effie, I'm talking about a million dollars here for Gled's child."

I could easily get her to go to two. It was like a book deal. And don't forget another million for promotion.

"What if it isn't Gled's child?"

"A fifty percent chance is good enough for me."

I began to wonder how she'd found me. If it was through the Martha connection, that would be bad. If Martha knew I'd kept the child, then Alan for sure knew too.

"Janice, how did you find me?"

"I hired a detective."

"It's too bad you didn't call me earlier today—before I got married."

"What?"

"To Gled." I joyfully pictured the blood draining out of her face. It was a better image than my flinging her out of her high-rise window by satellite *chi.* "Yes. Lucky Gled. He's got both me and the baby. And lucky baby. She hasn't got you for an adoptive parent."

"He wouldn't marry you without telling me!" Janice's voice quavered. She was more upset about being out of the loop than about our being married. "He's crazy now, Effie. He's not himself at all. Of course you know he just married you for the child. Oh hell, I'm still glad for him. I am. Effie, let's bury the hatchet."

"You're the hatchet," I pointed out.

"Don't tell Gled about this telephone call. Please." The *please* came out like a word she'd never said before, never even practiced.

Now was the time to bring up the million dollars again. She could pay for my silence. I'd give half to my mom and a quarter to each of my sisters. Wait a minute. What did that leave me?

"Sorry, Janice. I'm not going to begin my marriage keeping secrets." (Except for the major secret that I was already married.) "Anyhow, what the hell, you were just trying to buy him a baby to help him out. Nothing to be ashamed about. Goodbye. I've got to go. It's my wedding night."

"Hi, Mom. It's Effie."

"Hi, love. Did Gled find you?"

"Yes."

"I had to tell him. The poor guy."

"That's okay. Now he's flown back to Boston because Danny's come out of his coma."

"That's wonderful!"

"He wants to be the father of my child."

"Maybe he is."

"It doesn't matter, really. But it's nice for the baby to have a dad. We got married."

"What?"

"I thought Danny was dead from the way he told me about it and I felt so bad for him we got married."

"But, Effie, sweetheart, it's a felony."

"I knew it was against the law, but I thought it was more a church thing. Are you sure it's not a misdemeanor?"

"I think it's two years in prison, Effie."

"And I wouldn't get off for good behavior either. I'd get more for bad behavior."

"How can you joke?"

"Well, who's going to tell? I mean, who would turn me in?"

"Your husband would. When he finds out about the other husband. If he doesn't murder you first."

"Mom, don't take this so seriously. No one back East even needs to know about the marriage—although Lynn and Janice both know already. I had to tell Janice because she was trying to buy my baby out from under me to give to Gled."

"Oh, Effie, where did I go wrong? And you're not even working on your thesis, are you? How are you going to support yourself and the baby?"

"Who needs a job with two husbands? Bye, Mom. I'm going back to Bolinas, so you can call me there. I figure you should plan to come out in three weeks. Can you do that?"

"Effie, I've had the ticket for months. I look at it every day."

"Any word from Alan?"

"Not a peep. Nor from his mother. Not since Danny's accident."

"Okay. I've got to go."

"Take care of yourself. Love from the girls."

"My love to them."

"Hi, Effie."

"Hi, Gled. How's Danny?"

"He doesn't know me. 'This is your father,' Lynn told him and he just looked at me. Then he said, 'Hi.' It was horrible. It was worse than the coma. Imagine . . . imagine your mother or sister looking at you like a stranger and saying 'Hi' with no inflection."

"Gled, you have got to stop thinking of yourself. Try to put yourself in Danny's poor shattered little mind. What does it matter if he doesn't know you yet? What matters is that your wonderful little boy is alive and that he's mending."

"He's walking around, but he's so tottery."

"Of course he's tottery! What do you expect?"

"Lynn says I'm no help—sitting there looking at him with what she calls my 'gloom-and-doom expression.' "

"Go fly an airplane somewhere."

"I think I'd better. Are you okay without me?"

"I'm fine. I'm here with the birds."

"Tell me about a bird."

"I'll tell you about the California Woodpecker."

"I'm all ears."

"They live in families of ten or twelve birds, but only one or two pairs get to breed. The others in the group help the parents raise the young. This kind of communal breeding is scarce in the bird kingdom."

"But not in the human kingdom, where Emma, Ellie, Edna, and Gled will all help. I should change my name to Ed."

"And Danny will help too," I said, reminding him that his

son was a member of our family, even though he said "Hi" with no inflection. "So the family group stores acorns in decaying trees and they know to the centimeter how many acorns fit in a given hole, unlike a mouse, say, who will try endlessly to fit a big chunk of Emmentaler into a hole fit only for grated Parmesan. The woodpeckers hoard big-time, sometimes up to twenty thousand acorns, under the misapprehension that it's going to be a harsh winter. Then they have to expend a lot of energy protecting their acorn caches from pilferers, mainly squirrels. In the meantime, they eat fruit, nuts, and insects. Their beak is chisel-shaped for woodcutting purposes. As well as using it for pecking out grubs and insects, they chisel their nests out of the tree. The amazing thing is their cylindrical tongue, which is twice as long as the length of their head! At the end is a hard point with barbs on the sides."

"Ouch."

"It's a dislodging instrument."

"I'll go tell Danny."

"Yes, tell Danny. He'll love the tongue part. When it's not being used, it's coiled up inside the head."

"You're wonderful."

"You are too."

Gled was wonderful. Were it Alan I was telling about the woodpecker, he'd have wandered off for a drink halfway through or simply said, "That's enough about Woody for now."

Still, I was wondering a lot about how Alan was. I was tempted to call, but decided it was better to let sleeping dogs lie.

{18} Push Door

Two and a half weeks later, I was in Bolinas and had spent the day at the Point Reyes Bird Observatory. Before Gled left, he bought me an old Honda Civic, so if the labor pains came when I was in Bolinas, I could head for San Francisco and make it to the hospital in time. This car was so old it could go in a car museum as the first Japanese car in America, along with the Toyota Gled kept at the quarry, both of them yellow like his Ford convertible. I'd gotten a California driver's license easy as pie and was feeling quite the grown-up, owning something bigger than a suitcase for the first time in my life. At this point in my third trimester, I wasn't much for walking. Still, after a long day at the PRBO, I was restless, so, before returning to the lagoon house, I decided to take a hike along the Palo Marin trail, which followed the high cliffs along the shore. Gled was going to be arriving in Bolinas that evening, but I still had a couple of hours.

A hundred yards along the trail I spotted a rustic rest room and thought I'd better avail myself of it, as I seemed to need to do about every hour and a half. Normally, when out in the wild,

I would simply squat down behind a tree, but my squatting days were over for the next few weeks. The rest room was off the trail a way, down a little path.

The door opened inward and remained ajar, being still swollen from the winter and spring rains. Not thinking, I gave it a push, forgetting the power of my push, and it closed fully into the jamb. There was no lock on the door to worry me and I sat down and went about my business.

The toilet faced the door. That was when I noticed that the door had no knob or handle or anything with which to pull it open again when I was through and ready to take my leave.

I wiped myself and stood up, restoring my clothes to their correct wearing position, trying to quell the first feelings of anxiety that, if not contained, would escalate into full-blown panic.

Of course there was no window except high above the door and nothing to stand on to get to the window except the sink, which was attached to a different wall nowhere nearby. The door was tight against the jamb all the way around, except for a gap on the top near the outside corner (unreachable) and on the bottom edge near the hinge. The gap there was wide enough to get my fingers through and grasp it on the other side, but, being where it was, it did me no good. The door wouldn't budge.

There was a small hole where the handle, when it existed, had been bolted. It was about the size of my little finger and useless.

My worst fears vis-à-vis rest rooms had been realized.

I panicked. I cried. "Help, help!" until I was hoarse. This was not a well-traveled trail during the week and it was already late in the day. Still, "Help, help!" I cried. Someone might hear me and they weren't going to hear me if I didn't yell. I had to get the attention of any passing hiker or bird-watcher who didn't need to go to the bathroom.

I was completely unbalanced and out of control, a state of mind with no benefits. I tried to calm myself and somewhere inside my fear-smitten brain, through all the noise of the adrenaline rush cascading through my body and roaring in my ears, I remembered T'ai Chi.

Totteringly, I began the form. There wasn't much room, but I recollected my teacher saying she could do it in an airplane rest room. This was much bigger. I went through the form once, twice, three times. It worked like magic. By the end of the third round, I was not only calm and collected, I was illuminated. I had a brilliant idea.

I would go into the back of the toilet and take out a piece that would fit through the hole in the door. I would make a hook of it with which I could pull the door open. I whipped off the top of the toilet and unscrewed the iron piece that held the bulb. It was about six inches long. I inserted about two inches of it into the sink drain for purchase and bent it to a right angle. Now I had my hook! I put it through the hole in the door. However, it didn't leave me much to grasp at my end, and it was so thin that when I pulled on it, it slipped through my increasingly sweaty hands. The door didn't move a centimeter. It might as well have been cemented to the jamb. I pulled, I yanked. My hands were getting cramped into claws from trying to grasp the ungraspable. Finally my efforts simply ended in straightening out the hook. It was hopeless. By now almost two hours had gone by: a half hour of yelling, a half hour for the three forms, almost an hour to execute the brilliant idea. Now what? Do the form again and get another idea? No way.

That's when I felt the first pain.

Oh great.

In my wildest fears about getting locked in a public rest room, I never thought it would be on the edge of the continent, three thousand miles from home, on a rarely walked trail in a little-visited national park when I was almost nine months pregnant and going into labor. Oh yeah, and don't forget to add when it was getting dark.

I sat down on the toilet and cried. I began to rue the fact that I hadn't made friends in Bolinas who would form a posse to come looking for me. One of the reasons I'd wanted to come to California was to be open, talkative, and friendly. Instead I'd carried closed-mouthed, hard-bitten, nose-in-the air New England with me, looking down on the Bolinasites just because they smoked dope and didn't take showers. I hated myself. I had this coming to me.

When I got tired of that, I timed the pains. They were still between five and eight minutes apart, not regular, and my water hadn't broken. Maybe it was a false labor.

Then I couldn't time the pains anymore because it was too dark to see my watch. Then it was pitch black. Then my water broke.

Now I wasn't just scared of being locked in, I was scared of the cold, the dark, the pain, and the sounds of night creatures rustling and scampering about. This was mountain lion country and I actually began developing the crazy added fear that a lion could jump through the window over the door and eat me up, maybe because it was better than imagining dying in childbirth on the cement floor. However it was I died, it would probably all come out about my being a bigamist.

That's how a bigamist always gets found out. Because he suddenly has to go to the hospital and both wives come to see him and they walk into each other and say, "Who the hell are you?" Or they're at the funeral and look around to see who the bitch is sobbing louder than she is and getting all the attention. The reason my mind had reversed the sexes was it's always men who are the bigamists not women.

Mom's right, I thought. Where did she go wrong?

I heard some steps and then a thumping at the door. I froze.

I shrank into the corner where I was standing. I cowered. Some night-wandering rapist killer was after me now.

But wait. So what? At least I'd get out of this hell hole.

Yell, Effie. Yell. Now was the time for "Help, help!" if there ever was one.

I couldn't. My larynx was closed with fear. The call of the crane was silenced. I was struck mute.

A beam of light flashed through the gaps. "Effie?" came a voice. "Effie? Are you in there?" It was Gled.

I threw myself at the door. "Yes," I croaked. "I'm in here. Yes," I whispered hoarsely, scrabbling at my side of the door so he'd hear the scrabbles if not the paltry voice. "The door opens inward. Push."

{19} Push Baby

"Push!" said the firefighter.

We were at the Stinson Beach firehouse. That was as far as we got from the Palo Marin trail on the way to San Francisco. Stinson Beach was a coastal village of around a thousand people at the foot of Mount Tamalpais.

It had taken Gled a while to open the rest room door. Pushing, shoving, kicking didn't do the trick. He had to run at it full tilt and give it the old shoulder quite a few times before it was dislodged. By then my pains had accelerated to two minutes apart, regular as a heartbeat. We headed out, but by the time we came to Stinson Beach with ten miles of mountain road ahead before the open stretch to the city, the baby was crowning. We decided to see how the firehouse felt about an on-site delivery.

We were in high spirits. Gled was so happy to have rescued me and I to be rescued that the birth pains seemed negligible. After what I'd gone through, having a baby would be child's play. It was a lark. I was so relaxed and happy that I hardly felt a thing. Fear causes tension, which causes pain, and I'd used up all my fear in the rustic rest room. It was no time at all, I'd hardly stretched out, when we got to the push part and the baby started coming. The volunteer firefighter who was an emergency medical technician was soon replaced by a volunteer firefighter doctor. They told Gled to repair to the Sand Dollar bar next door, but he stuck around. He wanted to see Danny's little brother be born.

I have to admit I allowed myself a few screams there at the end, just for the drama of it all and because it helped with the pushing and because, well, for a minute, the pain was totally excruciating, but only for a minute, maybe ten, and then my baby came into the world. She came out of my own little body into our oxygen-laden sphere, into the good salty air of Stinson Beach, another generation in a long line of Crackalbee coastal dwellers, and it was the miracle mothers always say it is. Life going on. A complete new person taking her first gasp of air and vocalizing for the first time. I took her in my arms, tears of joy streaming down my face. The only thing missing was Mom.

Gled was there, but when I turned to him, I caught a downcast expression before he summoned up a loving smile. I knew what he was thinking. He was thinking it wasn't Danny's little brother because it was a girl and because, in all her pinkness and blondness, she probably wasn't even his child.

"Hi, Mom, it's Effie, calling from Stinson Beach."

"It's three A.M.! Is it the baby?"

"Yes. A little girl. Her name is Corinne. She's healthy and beautiful and I feel great. No problems. I only wish you were here."

"I'll change my ticket and get on the plane today. The girls are coming groggily down the hall. I'll let you tell them."

"Mom, you have to call us 'the women' now that we've had a baby."

"Here the women are."

"Effie, is it you? This is Edna and Ellie, heads together, sharing the receiver."

"Well, it finally happened. I got locked in a rest room."

"No!"

"Yes. In a national park. The door was wedged shut and there was no handle to pull it open."

"Oh God! Poor Effie. Your worst fears come true."

"Three hours!"

"What a nightmare."

"I was crazy with fear. Darkness came . . ."

"No!"

"And then I went into labor."

"I can't stand it!"

"Meanwhile, Gled arrived in Bolinas and couldn't find me. Luckily, someone told him I was at the bird observatory. He saw my car in the parking lot. He started down the trail, which is along these eroding cliffs at the edge of the ocean. California's falling into the sea at the rate of about three feet a year. He expected the worst. But he knew to look for a rest room first . . ."

"But what about the labor? Was it false?"

"By the time Gled broke in, it didn't feel a bit false. We headed for San Francisco but decided we wouldn't make it over the mountain. Stinson Beach has a volunteer fire department but no one was there. I called 911 from a phone booth outside and a firefighter came instantly. Volunteer is better than professional because then he can be a doctor too, which was who came next. The firehouse was just big enough to contain an engine and an ambulance. There was no place to lie down, so he put me in the ambulance on the little cot. Everything was spanking clean and they had an obstetrical and a pediatric kit on board. It's a baby girl."

"Effie! Congratulations! Are you all right? Is she?"

"We're both great. Her name is Corinne. That's the name of the wonderful woman who owns the Bolinas house."

"What about the baby's last name?"

"Don't ask. Well, I have to sleep now."

"In the ambulance?"

"Now we're in the motel next door. Goodbye, Corinne's aunties. We love you."

"Hi, Danny. It's Effie. You don't remember me, but I took care of you last summer and we were good buddies."

"I'm sorry."

"Honey, don't be. Don't even think of sorry."

"Dad told me you guys got married."

"Right. And last night we had a baby."

"Already?"

"Well, we made the baby last summer, of course. It takes nine months."

"I think I knew that."

"Anyhow, I wanted to tell you that you have a baby sister. Her name is Corinne. Last summer you said you really wanted a baby brother."

"I did?"

"Yes, and I'm sorry we didn't deliver, but this is the next best thing, maybe actually the best thing. She'll love having a big brother to look out for her."

"Effie?"

"Yes."

"It's sort of neat because . . . well, me and Corinne . . . we'll both start remembering things at the same time. I mean, in a way, I've just been born too."

"Yes, Danny, honey, you have. It's wonderful. Your dad and I love you a lot. Goodbye."

Gled came out of the bathroom. "Why are you crying?"

"I just talked to Danny." I told Gled what Danny had said about being newborn along with Corinne.

"I feel like you called Danny behind my back," he said glumly, sitting down on the bed. His jacket was there where I'd rummaged through it for Danny's number. He looked at the jacket. He didn't look at Corinne, who slept beside me wrapped tightly in a cotton blanket like a little papoose.

"Would you have wanted me to call Danny?"

"No. Probably not. He doesn't know you, Effie."

"He doesn't know any of us! But we know him. We have to keep treating him like our beloved same old Danny. We do, Gled. If you let his memory loss get you down, you'll drift away from him. He had to know about his baby sister."

"If she is . . . ?"

"Gled, this is very bad of you if you're going to say what I think you're going to say."

"I'm sorry, Effie. I'm a mess."

"If you feel, now, that you've made a mistake marrying me, we'll get it annulled."

He lay down on the other side of Corinne, covering his eyes with his arm. "How can I be acting like this after the night you've been through? I'm the lowest. Effie, I love you and I promise to love Corinne as if she . . ."

"Good God in heaven!"

"I can't help it. I know she's not mine. I didn't think it would matter, but it does matter. I've lost my son and now I've lost my daughter."

I was angry, but I spoke calmly, even pleasantly, because I didn't want my baby to hear harsh words on her first day of life or on any day of her life if I could help it.

"You don't know she's not yours. I'm disgusted with you. Why don't you get out of here and leave us alone? I never want to see you again," I said pleasantly. "I'll raise Corinne on my own. I don't need you. I never did need you, except for last night in the rest room. I really needed you then and I'll always be grateful that you found me and opened the door. Otherwise, Corinne and I might both be dead. However, I guess saving your daughter's life doesn't mean anything to you and doesn't make her any more yours. You don't want to feel good about yourself. You just want to feel sorry for yourself. I hate people like you." The more I wanted to scream at him, the softer my voice got. "And treating Danny like he isn't even a person. You should be ashamed."

He uncovered his face and looked at me. "I am ashamed. I am deeply ashamed. Please forgive me. I've never been good at being a husband. Ask Lynn."

"You are very good at being a father. That I know. That's all I'm asking." I looked meaningfully from Corinne's beautiful rosy sleeping face to his darkly troubled one. My eyes said, *Just look at her. How can you look at her and not love her? She's wholly cherishable.* He looked at her and I could see he felt nothing. He didn't love her. He couldn't help it. It was the strangest thing. It wasn't even that he might not be the father. Nor was it that he had wanted so much for her to be Danny's little brother. I think he'd actually wanted her to be Danny himself, beginning again. In his grief-stricken, unhinged, inconsolable mind, he'd thought I was carrying Danny. But Danny *was* beginning again, at the same time as Corinne. He'd said so himself.

"Have you called Janice?" I asked gently. Maybe it would do him good to talk to the hated, million-dollar, baby-buying Janice. She was the one he was closest to, who understood him. He needed understanding now and I was fresh out of it. Notwithstanding my gentle voice, I could have strangled him.

He lit up. "I'll call Janice," he said. "I'll call from the booth so as not to disturb you. And then I'll bring back some breakfast for us. Okay. I love you, Effie. Can you say that you love me?"

"Hell, no." I didn't look at him so I wouldn't relent. Then I relented a little. "Maybe later I'll say I love you. If all goes well." How could I love someone who didn't love my child who was maybe his child? That's why I stopped loving Alan. It's a perfect reason not to love someone any longer, if you ask me.

But I had to remind myself that what Gled had gone through was comparable to my experience in the rustic rest room, only it was four months instead of three hours! Four months of abandonment and fear.

"Go and call Janice," I said. "I love you."

I've never been a woman chary with her I-love-yous.

"Janice?"

"Gledforth! What's the news?"

"A baby girl. Born at midnight in the Stinson Beach firehouse."

"Congratulations. Mother and child doing well?"

"They're great."

"You don't sound so great yourself. Were you up all night?"

"Somehow the whole event has thrown me. It all seems too much for me."

"Do you mean the marriage to a relative stranger or the child that might not be yours?"

"I feel very close to Effie. Effie's wonderful and I love her, but I guess it's too much on top of Danny's trouble. Maybe I feel like I've lost Effie to her baby, that all her love will be for the baby now. I don't know. I'm all mixed up. And it's true. I don't feel like the baby's mine. She's very blonde."

"Do you want me to try to find out about the other man?"

"Absolutely not. Christ, you hire detectives like other women buy clothes."

"I buy a lot of clothes too, but it's nowhere near as satisfying."

"I don't want to know anything about the other man. If I want to know, all I have to do is ask Effie."

"One of her sisters is blonde."

"How do you know that?"

"From the detective I hired to find out where Effie was. All he did was talk to her sister. I could have done that myself and saved a thousand dollars."

"Or you could have asked me. It pisses me off. Why did you do that?"

"You mean Effie didn't tell you."

"No."

"I'm impressed."

"So you tell me."

"Well, it was when Danny seemed hopelessly lost. I thought I'd try to get Effie's baby for you. I was going to adopt."

"You are amazing. I'm incredibly touched."

"Don't be. I had to do something. I felt so helpless. Never mind. Forget about it. Gled, I think you need some help. I think you should have therapy."

"Pilots don't have therapy."

"Right. I forgot."

"I already feel better just reminding myself I'm a pilot and own all that wide blue acreage."

"You're acreage in Lanesville is pretty nice too."

"And it's almost summer. I hope I can get Effie to come back for the summer. She's getting pretty wedded to this coast. Meanwhile, I've got to go and find us some breakfast. Bye for now."

"Look, just hold the baby in your arms. You have to bond."

{20} Step Back to Ride the Tiger

"Hello, is this Alan Croy?"

"Speaking."

"My name is Gled Saltonstall."

"Oh . . . yes."

"I got your name by tracking down your car license. We both live in Lanesville in the summer."

"I know. I'm very sorry about your son."

"It's my son I'm calling about. I've been in a fog ever since his accident, but last weekend I was in Lanesville and I saw your Porsche and it came back to me how you almost crashed into me and my son last summer on High Street."

"Sorry about that."

"You were going much too fast and in the middle of the road. I had to swerve into the bushes. I called you a jerk and you gave me the finger."

"Deplorable. I'm sorry. My wife, Jane, says driving brings out the worst in me. I'm beginning to think she's right."

"Your car appears to have a recent paint job."

"No, it's a few years old."

"I guess I can find out. You see, my son's skateboard had green paint on it. That's all we know about the hit-and-run."

"Surely you're not accusing me?"

"I'm looking into it."

"Well, look elsewhere."

"You were in Lanesville for Thanksgiving weekend."

"You're completely mad."

"And you're a known reckless driver."

"Goodbye."

"Hello?"

"Gled Saltonstall just called up and accused me of being the hit-and-run driver responsible for his son's death."

"He didn't die, darling."

"That's good."

"And he's out of the coma now too. I've been staying in touch with the hospital all these months. He's home."

"Here in Lanesville?"

"No, with his mother, Lynn, in Lynn. Isn't that funny, that she lives in a town of her same name?"

"Hilarious. And isn't it funny that Jane never mentioned he was divorced?"

"Not particularly. Everyone's divorced. But, Alan, what did he say?"

"That I was a known reckless driver who ran him off the road last summer and Danny's skateboard has green paint on it and he sees I've had my car repainted."

"Have you?"

"Three years ago. But I haven't put a scratch on it since. Pretty good, for a reckless driver."

"Maybe because you run people off the road before they can hit you?"

"Very funny."

"Well, darling, are you alarmed about this conversation with Saltonstall?"

"No, I'm angry. It's no fun being wrongly accused twice. Perhaps you remember your hysterical call last November on the same subject."

"I've apologized for that till the cows come home. You neither forgive nor forget. You're like your father that way. Have you been drinking?"

"Yes, I've been drinking. What else is there to do? School's over. Jane is over too, as far as I can tell. It's beginning to sound ridiculous my still telling people she's away researching her thesis after nine months. Did I say nine months? The baby would be born now. Our baby. It would be born and a month old if I'd let it live. You're right. I'm a murderer. Jane was a hit-and-run victim."

"I'm actually beginning to feel worried about you. I think I should come down to Lanesville and stay with you."

"I beg you not to."

"If only you would . . ."

"Work on my novel? Ha!"

"Darling, you made such a good beginning. I was blown away. Honestly. I want to talk to you about it."

"Goodbye."

"Jane, this is Martha."

"Martha, my goodness, what a surprise. How are you?"

"Not very well, dear. I'm calling from the Gloucester hospital . . ."

"Oh dear. Take your time. Is it Alan?"

"Yes . . ."

"Did he have an accident? Martha, try to talk."

"Suicide attempt. Carbon monoxide poisoning. I found him in the garage. Thank God I came down to the shore. He was upset and drinking and I had a feeling. Jane, do you know about Danny?"

"Yes, I do."

"Well, Danny's father called Alan and accused him of the hit-and-run."

"No!"

"Yes. And, Jane? I think he might have done it. I've thought so from the first."

"No, Martha. Alan might have an accident, but he'd never run from it. He wouldn't leave a hurt little boy on the street. Never."

"He looks so ghastly. He's absolutely gray. He looks about a hundred years old. Jane, will you come? Please. He needs you more than you can possibly imagine."

"Of course. I'll come right away."

"Thank you with all my heart. If you'll let me know your flight, I'll meet you at the airport. Here's my Visa card number for the ticket."

In the airport, before boarding, I went through the form to relax and energize myself for the flight. Corinne was in a baby pack on my chest. She loved the movements. She was a month and a half old now, a good baby. Mom had come out and spent three weeks with us. I'd moved from the boardinghouse to a one-bedroom apartment on Russian Hill. Gled had taken a job flying a private Learjet for a wealthy and mysterious local person and this allowed him to spend more time with us, as well as providing him with an actual salary, but he made a beeline for Danny whenever he could.

He was devoted and loving to me and trying his best to be so with Corinne, but Danny's memory loss weighed on him. It was as if so long as Danny did not remember who he was, he only half-existed. He was only walking through the part. I could understand because when I first came to San Francisco, I would go for days—sometimes for weeks—with no one who knew me and I began to not be so sure about who I was or if I was. It helps to have people around who know you and love you to feel you are a live, unique person, not a wraith.

Danny didn't know him and Lynn acted like she hated him and Janice was busy making money. He had lots of male friends, but they were daredevils like himself, so with them he had to keep up a front. I tried to give him a lot of love and attention the rare times when I saw him, although with Corinne still newborn, we couldn't get wholly physical.

Gled had flown to Hawaii when I got the call from Martha, so I'd left him a note and an outgoing message on my machine saying that he could reach me at the quarry, as I'd gone to Lanesville to see an ailing friend. Gled had been trying to persuade me to come to the quarry for the summer (it was now June), so he'd be delighted that I'd repaired thence. I'd alerted the Flanagans about my arrival.

In the airport, when I got to the part of the form called Step Back to Ride the Tiger, I held it. With the weight back on my right leg, my left foot takes a half-step back and rests with just my toes touching the ground. Hands are open: right hand by right shoulder in a stop sign, the other down by the left knee. It is a relaxed position preparatory to the most intricate T'ai Chi maneuver—performing a full circle on the right leg, then raising the leg into a shoulder-high circular kick called the Lotus Kick.

I guess I paused in this position, realizing the intricate maneuvers that lay ahead as I prepared to return to the East Coast and what I suppose was my real life. It would be capricious to say that my time in California had been for the birds—after all, my baby had been born—but it had definitely been a suspended period wherein I had let events carry me forth without coming to grips with what I was doing and why I was doing it. Now I was going full circle back to Alan—whether to perform the Lotus Kick or not remained to be seen. It certainly wasn't in me to kick a man when he was down. It's against all T'ai Chi principles.

Martha met me at the gate at Logan International as I struggled along with my carry-on bags (now carry-off). Always so proud of being a light packer, I'd had to relinquish my lighthearted traveling style for Corinne's needs. How anyone so tiny can take up so much suitcase beats me. Martha looked chic in her slapdash way, wearing beige linen slacks and a black hooded sweatshirt accentuating her light flyaway hair. I wore Corinne in a pack over a blowsy blue tentish dress.

"Oh, Jane, it's the baby! You've had the baby! Oh, my darling girl, good for you! What a blessing for us all! This is just what Alan needs to turn him around."

"Really?"

"Oh, just look at her. What a treasure! What an absolute beauty! Don't you think she looks a little like me?"

"Not at all."

Martha laughed. I began to remember how much I liked her. She had grabbed all of the bags and was whisking me down the corridors and escalators to where she'd illegally parked her Lincoln town car. She'd probably put on consular plates in order to do so.

"But are you saying you think Alan will be glad?" I asked as I settled into the passenger seat.

"My dear. That's what this suicide attempt was all about. He hasn't been able to forgive himself for one minute that he asked you to kill the child."

"Please don't say such things in front of Corinne. I don't want her ever to know that."

"Of course. Forgive me." Martha looked chastened.

"But why didn't Alan say so?" I persisted. "To me."

"How could he? He thought the baby was d . . ." She pressed her lips together. "He thought it was a *fait accompli.* It would be salt in the wound to express his regrets. Oh, Jane, this is so wonderful. I can't tell you."

But she did tell me, rattling happily away as we covered the forty miles to Cape Ann. Then she asked for my take on California.

"It's wonderful. The winter is warm. It's the first winter when I didn't slip and fall down and break my ass on an icy sidewalk. There's no slush. There are flowers instead. The people are friendly. They smile and say hello. Some of them aren't very smart, but even the smart ones don't bother to act like they are because they're not trying to impress. Everyone wears jeans. There are no snobs. There are no loathsome and vile people. The produce is wonderful all winter. Fresh orange juice everywhere you look. Millions more birds."

"That's enough," she said in the spirit of her son, for, like him, she preferred to be the primary talker. "I must prepare you," she said as we drove the rocky road to the shore, "Alan looks absolutely ghastly. It's the alcohol poisoning along with the gas poisoning. Is it all right to say 'poisoning' in front of Corinne?"

"I guess so. I don't think she knows three-syllable words yet."

We both laughed and Corinne made what seemed like a tiny chuckle in her sleep.

The Atlantic Ocean greeted me, green and wavy, whitecapped and begulled. The real ocean, I thought, my loyalties shifting already to the present coast. It was high tide and waves slapped and swirled against the granite boundary of coastal rocks. No erosion here! In the late-afternoon light, the water had an angry glitter that the Pacific, living up to its name, didn't have. This was the ship-swallowing ocean, the destroyer, the mother of all maelstroms.

"He'll be in the bedroom," Martha whispered as we entered the house. "Shall I take the baby for now? It might be too much of a shock to see her as well as you."

"Okay. I eased her out of the pack and into Martha's arms. She was awake now and looked up at Martha trustingly. Martha took her like an old hand, which surprised me. It had been twenty-eight years since Alan was Corinne's size and I was sure he'd had a nanny. I unstrapped the pack and marched off to Alan's room.

He was lying on the bed, staring at the ceiling. He looked all puffy and bloated and, as Martha had said, gray, the color of exhaust. It was a pitiful sight. It wrung my heart. Despite the sea breezes through the open window, the room was stinky.

I sat down on the bed. "Your mom asked me to come and I came at once."

"Jane, is it really you? You look so big. Your breasts . . ."

"Alan, I'm sorry you were feeling so bad that you had to do this. I wish I had known. It's my fault for cutting off contact."

"Look, it's all a big misunderstanding. It was not a suicide attempt. I just had too much to drink, decided to go for a drive, and fell asleep at the wheel before I got out of the garage."

"Alan, Martha told me you'd connected a vacuum hose from the car exhaust to the window."

"A vacuum hose? Really?"

I nodded. "There aren't any rubber hoses around, since you don't have a garden. It was actually quite clever of you, in your drunken stupor, to think of the vacuum hose."

"Especially since I've never vacuumed in my life. I wonder if there was an attachment at the end of it and, if so, whether it was for floor or carpet? There might be some symbolism in that."

Even though he was making jokes, his voice was completely dead. It was like a computer voice. His puffy, sagging face had no expression at all.

"The window was open where you'd put the hose in the car," I explained, "so you'd stuffed newspapers around it. It was a pretty serious attempt, I'd say."

"Unlike the secondary-type attempt, the old 'cry for help.' "

"You'd never cry for help. Unfortunately." I leaned over and kissed his poor old face. "Your mother must have arrived within minutes or you'd be a goner."

"Why are you making such a point of all this?"

"I don't know."

Was I kicking a man when he was down? I hoped not. I guess I just didn't want him to fool himself or, worse, to try to fool me.

"Did you come all this way just to tell me about the vacuum cleaner? You haven't even said whether it was a Hoover or an Electro-lux."

"I came because I was concerned about you. And because I wanted you to meet Corinne."

I was about to rise and get her when Martha, on cue, stepped into the room. It kind of took the moment away from me for her to be holding the child, but I had to say it was a wonderful picture. Martha had this great tremulous smile on her face and was displaying Corinne as if she were the Baby Jesus.

Alan, terminally inert only moments before, sprang from the bed. Tears started pouring down his face. He stretched out his arms beseechingly and Martha put Corinne into them. Corinne, who had been in no one's arms but mine for the last three weeks, seemed delighted to be passed around like a football. She looked up at Alan and I almost expected her to say, "Dada." Damned if I wasn't crying too. Everyone was crying but Corinne, who, as a baby, was supposed to cry but who, in fact, to date, had, I swear, only done so once or twice.

"This is the happiest day of my life," Alan said.

{21} Riding the Tiger

A few days later I was still riding the tiger and so far it was a smooth ride, probably because Gled still wasn't in the picture and wouldn't arrive at the quarry for two more days. The tiger was just walking along, carrying me on his back like a faithful Saint Bernard, but at any moment it could start to leap, growl, claw, climb trees, and maybe even turn us all into melted butter.

We were in the living room in front of the fire. Alan lay on the couch with Corinne stomach-down on his chest. She was holding her head up and Alan was praising this new move of hers, extolling her fine neck muscles. He was totally crazy about her and, needless to say, it warmed my heart after Gled's way of just giving her the fish eye as if she were an intruder.

Since the living room was half the size of Gled's, it couldn't, like his, contain a grand piano and whereas his furniture was all old and slipcovered in faded pastels and placed on priceless rugs, Martha's decor was culled from different winter homes she'd had during her life and nothing quite went together. The paintings on the walls were adequate landscapes and seascapes, while Gled had subtle unexpected treasures like the Hiroshige and an actual small Klee and two Picasso lithographs, along with some fine family portraits, and, of course, the fabulous library.

Still, like her own way of dressing, Martha's house had a slapdash who-gives-a-shit style, was colorful and cozy, and, through the big picture windows, had the ultimate decoration of the great ship-swallower in all its moods and colors.

It was amazing and frightening how comfortable I felt being here with Alan and Martha, frightening that I was so adaptable. The other coast, the other marriage, began to recede in my mind, as if it had only been a trip, a sightseeing tour, a side step, and now I was back home and going forward along my rightful path.

I wanted to shake myself, kick myself, but I was too fat and happy in my armchair watching Alan play with Corinne, listening to Martha be amusing. I certainly hadn't had many laughs in the last almost-year. Instead of remembering my bird-watching adventures, what loomed large was my being a pregnant cleaning lady, living monastically, counting pennies until the nightmare solitary labor in a national park privy, then being locked into a joyless marriage with a grief-stricken man.

Alan was beginning to look like his handsome old self again and on the strength of this, Martha, sitting down with a martini, said, "Alan, I have some news."

I hadn't seen a martini the entire time I was in California. Alan cocked an eye her way and I moved uneasily in my chair, always slightly leery of news, especially when combined with martinis. And although she was sipping at it in a fairly patrician way, there wasn't much space between sips. She might as well have slugged it down and been done with it, Effie-style. I felt she needed the courage it would give her. Maybe she'd slugged one down in the kitchen so she could sip genteely at this one. That's what I'd do.

"You know how much I liked the start of your novel. Well, I

decided to give it to my agent to see if she couldn't get you some sort of deal because, well, nothing I said seemed to encourage you enough to go on with it. I feel there's nothing quite so encouraging as money. It shows real interest on a publisher's part."

"But I only had thirty pages. How could you make a deal with that? And no outline. And no publishing history!"

"I took the liberty of writing some more pages for you. You'd spoken so much about the novel over the years, it was a simple task and, as you know, I have a certain amount of practice replicating people's styles. I stayed utterly true to you, darling, you can rest assured."

"Jane, you'd better take Corinne. I have to sit up. This is going to be very hard to listen to without a drink." (He'd been forbidden to drink. Doctor's orders.) "I'm already incredibly angry. This is a complete invasion!"

"For Corinne's sake, please don't shout," I said. "I promised her she'd grow up not hearing any angry words." I took Corinne in my arms and decided to nurse her from one of my enormous breasts, which were dripping milk already. Her mouth tugged away and I felt physical pleasure in both breasts and in my uterus, as well as the emotional pleasure of seeing her sweet face and little hands, feeling the warm weight of her against me, the happiness of our being still attached to each other by nipple and tongue if not umbilicus.

"Exactly how many pages did you add to my thirty?"

"Well, seventy. I figured we needed a hundred to make a sale. It's called a partial."

"And?"

"And then I enhanced your image a bit because, sad to say, these days one is selling the author almost more than the book. I told Janice to bruit it about that this was the return of the WASP because all the good deals are going to Third Worlders and I think it's high time for a backlash. The handsome, young, blond, highly educated, interestingly depraved, tennis-playing, sailing, ne'er-do-well WASP.

Alan put his head in his hands. "Go on," he said wearily.

"Then, to add a little panache, I made you French. Alain Croix."

I couldn't help it. I started to laugh. Martha looked at me gratefully and laughed a little too. Alan still had his hands over his face. Corinne pulled away from my nipple to look at me. I put her on my shoulder for a burp.

"After all, Alan, you did spend your first five years in France." Martha turned to me, put down her martini, and spread her hands. "Jane," she said, "I so wanted him to grow up speaking French, and he did speak lovely French, perfect accent, but from the day we came home to the United States, he refused to talk it anymore. It was heartbreaking. However, it's all still there. I'm sure it can be accessed."

Alan, or Alain, stood up saying fiercely (but quietly for Corinne's sake), "So that I can drop French phrases during interviews. Sure. A five-year-old's conversation with a five-year-old's vocabulary—sublime sentences, such as: 'I need to pee-pee.' 'Are we almost there?' 'Let's play.' 'Can I have a candy?' "

Martha laughed. "Yes and lots of jokes about farting. Five-year-olds love farting jokes. However, darling, most people in the world have a vocabulary of one hundred and fifty words. Even at five, you were way ahead."

"Go on with your tale. I'm sure there's more."

"Actually, I called you X. Alain Croix. I love the two X's bracketing your name and it brings to mind F. Scott Fitzgerald, existentialism, and Generation X all at once. We'll call it an existentialist antimemoir. That's another thing the market is flooded with: memoirs. Time for a backlash on that too and a return to Sartre and Camus, real intellectuals. I tried to computer-scan a cigarette onto your photo, hanging from the corner of your mouth, your eyes squinting from the smoke, but no luck. I mean, where have the French been all these years? All the great fiction is coming from Japan, South America, India, and Leeds."

"X could be for Xavier," I contributed. "I like it."

"Yes," said Alain, "just to add a dash of Cuban. Maybe she could scan in a cigar."

Martha and I laughed merrily. All my disapproval of her criminal profession, her literary forgeries, now struck me as great fun. Having a baby had loosened me up. Or maybe being a bigamist had made me more understanding of a fellow felon.

"Xanadu would be nice," said Martha and we both fell about laughing again.

"Scan in some opium," I said gleefully, Xanadu being a reference to Coleridge's poem written under opium's salutary influence.

Alan was smiling in spite of himself.

"So did Janice make a deal?" I asked, figuring it was time to get to the heart of the matter. I gave Corinne the other breast. She'd had her burp and my shoulder was covered with expelled milk. I always forgot to put a diaper there. The truth was: I was a squalid mess these days. Short, fat, overbosomed, spotted damply here and there with drool and milk and pee, hair neglected, nails ragged. I could have been an ad for a woman unable to keep her husband—only my ad would have to say "unable to keep either husband." Martha made up for it by looking ultra-soignée in pale green silk, black sweatshirt slung over her shoulders like an exotic fur. If it's a mother's dream to outshine her daughter-in-law, she did. At least I only had one mother-in-law to outshine me; there was that to be said for my bigamy.

"Alan, you'd better sit down." Martha said. He did, after adding some small logs to the fire. Comparisons are onerous, but he was a much better fire-maker than Gled, not to mention a better father.

Martha spoke. "It's two million dollars—for this book and the next." Alan didn't hear the last part of the sentence. He'd fainted dead away onto the floor, but at least not from a standing position, so no harm done. I guess he wasn't as recovered as we thought. I myself was shocked. Corinne whimpered as she felt me stiffen. Again she pulled away from the nipple to look at me. I gave it back to her saying, "Never mind. It's not your business." She suckled on contentedly.

"Oh dear," said Martha. "What shall we do?"

"You tend to X.," I said, rising. "I'll put Corinne to bed."

When I came back downstairs a half hour later, Alan was reading the seventy purloined pages (stolen from his mind) and seemed absolutely riveted. With every page, he let loose some adjective like *great, fantastic,* and so on. Of course he was looking at the words through a two-million-dollar lens. Venality was triumphant. Worth that much money, the novel had to be great.

"You've done a hell of a job," he said to his mother. By tomorrow it would doubtless be *"I've* done a hell of a job," but Martha was used to that, I was sure.

"Are you ready to sign the contracts?"

"Bring them on."

All my merriment had turned sour. "Just a minute. Before you become world-famous, don't you think you'd better clear up this small matter of being a hit-and-run artist. It wouldn't look good on the publicity releases. Being a murderer is good publicity, we all know that, but there's just something about driving over a little boy and leaving him for dead that colors the whole image of the French intellectual, no matter how young, blond, and handsome. I don't think your publisher would like it."

"Jane's right," said Martha. She lit one of her rare cigarettes. She'd put down another martini or two and was starting to slur her words.

"I didn't do it," Alan said stonily.

"I'm sure you didn't. But Gled thinks you did. And there's

the suicide attempt. It will all get out. I'd hold off on the signature until it's cleared up."

"Jane's right," said Martha again.

"How do we clear it up?" Alan asked me.

"We find out who did it," I replied.

{22} Tiger Ride Gets Rough

"Hello, Lynn. This is Effie."

"Hello, Effie."

"How's Danny today?"

"He's pretty quiet. A friend of his came over this morning, but . . . well, it's very awkward. They had nothing to talk about, nothing to do. It doesn't help that I won't let him out of my sight. It's terrible to say, but I wish he were still in his coma. Then he could just lie there and be safe."

"Lynn, I'm at the quarry now. Gled's coming tomorrow. It would be so good for him if Danny could come and stay here for a day or two."

"I'm sorry, it's out of the question."

"He'll be safe, Lynn. We won't leave him alone. Please try to trust us."

"No. I'm too scared. Think of the quarry. How do we even know if Danny remembers how to swim? It's terrifying. And Gled . . . well, I won't talk about Gled, who was sleeping while Danny was lying bloody on the road."

"Gled feels that he's lost Danny."

"I can't help what he feels. I don't care what he feels. He has his new family."

"Lynn, I have to tell you, my baby means nothing to Gled. He won't even hold her. He'll hardly look at her."

"Well, I'm sorry about that, Effie, I am. Still . . . I guess you knew what you were buying into."

"All he thinks about is Danny. Maybe he thinks he's betraying Danny to love Corinne. I don't know."

"I never said he didn't love Danny with all his heart. He loved me that way too—once. He feels things strongly, I know, but I'm sick of his feelings. I just want Danny and me to be left alone."

"He's inconsolable. Without Danny in his life, he's only part of a person."

"I can't let Gled take him. I'm too scared."

"I want to see Danny too."

"Danny enjoys the talks he has with you on the phone. I know he got very attached to you last summer, Effie. However, I'm keeping him here and that's that. No sense discussing it any further."

"Hi, Ellie and Edna. Hi, women, it's Effie."

"Effie! When can we come see Corinne? We're dying."

"I'll let you know. Things are tricky around here and they're going to get trickier fast."

"Tell us everything."

"What can I say? Alan is recovering. He's sold his book for two million dollars, so that helps."

"No!"

"But I won't let him sign the contract until he's cleared of the hit-and-run rap I told you about."

"And Danny?"

"Still in the dark. I talked to Lynn and she said the most horrible thing . . ."

"What?"

"That she wished he were still in a coma so she wouldn't have to worry about him."

"Poor thing. She must be such an emotional mess, Effie. The strain she's been through. And she's all alone to deal. I'd be the same way. I'd Scotch-tape him to me."

"But how is he going to get better in an atmosphere like that? She won't let him come to the quarry. She's keeping him from Gled. Think how he feels."

"It's worse for her, Effie. Remember how you felt, locked in the rest room?"

"Nothing's as bad as that. She's got it easy."

"But think of being afraid every minute, even when you're sleeping. She probably gets up ten times a night to look at him."

"It can't touch the rest room ordeal."

"Oh yes, Effie. Oh yes it can!"

I was going back and forth from the quarry to the shore. I'd spent the first two nights with Alan and Martha until I felt that he was safe from harming himself, then decamped to the quarry, explaining to Alan that Gled had told me the room over the garage was mine any time and that Gled was currently not in residence.

"I don't much like your staying in my accuser's house."

"I don't care what you like or don't like. Don't think that just because I cared enough to come back, our marriage will blithely resume."

We were sitting down on the rocks, the three of us. I wanted Corinne to absorb the ocean, have it part of her consciousness: the light and color and sound, the lapping of waves and the mewling of gulls, the minute bubbling sound the seaweed made as the retreating tide released it to the element air, maybe even the scrabbling of crab legs in the tidal pools, the slinking along of snails. Who knew how much babies could hear before they decided to just attend to what concerned them. And smell. I wanted her little nostrils to drink in the fresh salt air with its negative ions, although I never understood why the negative ones were the good ones.

Alan was talking. "I'd do anything to get you back, Jane—you and Corinne. You can watch birds to your heart's content. Hell, we can go anywhere in the world to write, you your thesis, I my novel, just like we dreamed from the start. We're rich!"

He still didn't know how far I'd wandered from my thesis—so far that it was not only out of sight, it was out of mind. He didn't know that I wasn't even a bird-watcher, that since Corinne's birth, I'd only watched her.

"We're not rich yet," I reminded him, somewhat grimly, and then I wondered why I'd said "we," which I could tell he'd noticed and filed away gleefully. "Not until I find the hit-and-run driver."

"How do you propose finding the real perpetrator?"

"I'll talk to people. I feel like the village knows, maybe unconsciously, that it's one of them. Villages always know. And it couldn't have been a tourist. A tourist would not have been off the main route on a little side street with no shops on it. Anyhow, tourists don't come down here in late November."

Alan wasn't listening. He put an arm around me. "Let's go inside and put Corinne down and make love."

I have to admit I felt a pang of arousal, which I paused to enjoy before saying, "No."

"Are you waiting until you know I'm not the hit-and-runner?"

"I know you're not."

"Then why wait? What are we waiting for? Is it because of last fall and Corinne?"

"No."

"Then why? Just give me a reason. Is there someone else?"

"Yes."

"On the coast?"

"Yes." Gled was still on the coast.

"But you came here to be with me. You brought Corinne. How could there be anyone else if you were childbearing? You're making this up. Never mind. You probably want to be sure I didn't hit Danny—but you want me to think you believe me, so I won't commit suicide again. I don't blame you. We'll wait."

The next morning I discussed it with Mom—or tried to. She'd arrived at the quarry the night before when Corinne was asleep, and had been cooing over her constantly all morning. Between Alan and the two grandmothers, I hardly got to hold Corinne myself. At least I was the only one who could nurse her. Those minutes were ours, drawing sustenance and ease from each other. But it was hard to get Mom's attention. "Mom, put Corinne in my bedroom so I can talk to you and you'll listen."

"It looks bad for Alan," I explained when she returned halfway, giving me half of her attention. "He went into a depression right after the accident and he admits he felt like a murderer because he related Danny's death to the abortion."

"Yes, I can see that," Mom said while hovering by the bedroom door and craning her neck to see in.

"Mom, please come over here and sit by me. I need you."

She had gone all grandmothery: let her hair grow out gray and ceased to wear makeup. She looked wonderful. She even seemed thinner, as if I were wearing her weight for her. We'd traded figures.

She came and sat by me on the couch, giving me her undivided attention, which is what moms are for. No one can listen like a mother.

"Then," I continued, "there's the known fact that he's a terrible driver. Also, it doesn't look good that, after Gled accused him, he tried to take his life."

"His life would be ruined if it were true," Mom said. "Harvard would drop him. Everyone would. I sure would."

"Right. Finally there's the bit about the green paint that was on the skateboard and is similar to Alan's green car. Lynn destroyed the skateboard, so we can't match it up. There's no paint missing on the car, but he could have gotten it repainted. He says not."

"You could call all the car-painting places around. It would probably have been done the following week and green is at least more rare than some other colors."

"Gled thought of that. He got Janice to hire someone to get onto it. It seems an insuperable task, but maybe not."

"What do you honestly think, Effie?"

"I think if Alan hit someone, he'd step on the brakes and jump from the car and take care of the injured person. He wouldn't run from it. He wouldn't panic and keep going. But who would?"

Mom was thoughtful. "Say it was some old person who maybe didn't know what they'd done. Maybe they felt a bump and kept on going. Then it comes out about the hit-and-run and they just keep quiet. They're scared. I'd look for an old person with a green car."

"Yes."

"Talk to the locals. Maybe the locals are protecting one of their own from the rich summer people, protecting someone they love."

"That's my thinking."

Before I left the house to take Mom's advice, I found myself looking at the Hiroshige picture of the two cranes, one standing in the marsh, one spreading its wings. Ten months had passed since I first gazed on this picture. One day I'd left Alan for the West Coast of America and ended up in this house on the same day. Yet, I had gone to California. I had spread my wings. I'd begun to learn about the bird kingdom and, after nesting with sea elephants, I'd given birth to my child. What an incredible journey life was. What a flight! What a tiger ride!

I had dropped the briefly pleasing notion that I'd been a poor, pregnant, starving, put-upon cleaning lady the whole time, stumbling through the dreary days with broom, mop, and pail. Not true. I'd had a wonderful time. I'd lived life to the hilt, been courageous. And if my marriage with Gled hadn't been joyful, it was only because he was a suffering human being, going through a hard time, not because he was a spouter. I'd grown. Maybe I'd deepened, although probably not. But for sure I'd grown—from size six to size twelve.

After my talk with Mom, I spent the morning wandering around the village, looking for green cars, talking to whoever would listen. It was the same ground Gled had gone over. And over and over. But he was gaga with grief at the time and I was sharp as a tack. I felt like I could read minds. If I could identify a bird in flight, I could certainly identify a lie told right in my face, but there was just a lot of head-shaking and scratching, sighing, lip contortions, glasses-polishing, and the occasional nose-blowing, none of which were signs of deceit. No one knew anything. No one could figure it out. They were stumped. They'd say so-and-so had a green car, then qualify, saying he was away at the time or he didn't use his car in winter or he never took High Street. It was maddening.

I went into the coffee shop, had a grilled cheese sandwich and an ice tea with lemon. I thought of the old lady who'd driven me to the train station, whom I'd seen again here in the coffee shop on the day of my scene with Janice, the one who said, "Man in a hat." By God, she'd driven a green Chevy.

I asked the waitress, "Do you know the old lady who comes in here a lot, drives a green Chevy, doesn't say much, has a mole on her upper lip?"

"That's Elma."

Elma! One of my own family of stupid little E names.

"Does she live in Lanesville?"

"She's a summer person. Lives on the shore."

"It's summer now."

"Not really. Not until mid-June."

She could have come down for Thanksgiving. Gled and Janice did. Martha and Alan did, even though the house wasn't winterized. The only thing was: Elma was a really good driver, much better than Alan, almost as good as Gled. And her entire person smacked of integrity. Still, green car, that was the key, the only key we had.

I walked over to Alan's house by way of Lanes Cove, the rocks, and the shore road. Asking as I went, I found out which was Elma's house: a pretty white cottage with wraparound ocean-view porch and lots of petunias. But neighbors said she hadn't moved in for the season.

At Alan's, I stepped into the garage before going into the house. Martha's car and some rent-a-car were parked outside. Alan's Porsche had been inside since the night of his near death. It was a twenties garage, built for one car, a ladder going up to a storage room in the rafters.

There were shelves on the walls with tools and cans and bottles of cleaning agents and oils and the usual flotsam and jetsam of garages, among them a small, very small, probably half-pint can of paint the color of Alan's car. I opened it with a screwdriver. It didn't look new and it didn't seem to have been opened before. It didn't seem to have been used. It was quite full. I stirred it around. It was definitely Alan's green car paint. This was very bad. But if it was very bad, why would he have left it there on the shelf, plain as day?

I went into the house. There were voices in the living room. "Hello, Jane, darling," Martha greeted me. "Come and meet Janice, my agent and now Alan's agent too. She's come to see what the holdup is with the contracts. Janice, this is Alan's wife, Jane."

I froze. But Janice hardly gave me a glance. I couldn't figure it out until I remembered how tubby I was now and that I was introduced as Alan's wife, Jane, and therefore, to Janice, I couldn't possibly be her brother's slender little wife named Effie. It was a matter of context.

But then Martha remembered, "Oh, I forgot. You two know each other from last summer."

Now Janice did glance at me, but I made no impression. She had other things on her mind. Money. Martha continued to address me.

"Alan and I explained to Janice that the problem with the contract-signing is her own brother, but she doesn't think it matters."

Janice, long and lean, garbed in silk, with a great new haircut and teeth whiter and bigger than ever, waved her jeweled hand in the air, brushing the problem aside. "The accident is over and done with, a thing of the past," Janice told Alan. "Danny's fine. Nobody cares anymore. Forget it."

Fifteen percent of two million is three hundred thousand, I was thinking. Her cut.

"Gled cares," Alan said. "He's accused me."

"Only because it gave him a shock when he recently saw your Porsche and remembered a near accident with you last summer. But now he's checked it out with auto-body shops and found nothing to connect you." She pushed the papers at him. "Sign. It looks strange, your holding up the contracts. Of course I said nothing about your suicide attempt to the publisher . . ." This last came out as a veiled warning, but everything Janice said sounded like a warning.

"Alain, je pense que nous sommes dans une situation très difficile," Martha was alluding to the fact that the situation was damned tricky.

"Je pense qu'il fait necessaire que je fait vomir," Alan replied, accessing a childhood sentence, saying he thought it was necessary that he throw up.

Martha beamed, thrilled to hear French issuing from her Francothropic son's mouth at last, and I had to admit his accent was a marvel. He had the *r* down perfectly.

"Does Gled know about the suicide attempt?" Martha asked Janice.

"Yes."

"Great," said Alan bitterly. "He probably thought it was because he'd accused me of the hit-and-run."

"What *was* it about, by the way?" Janice asked inquisitively, not in an idle way, more in the spirit of the Spanish Inquisition. She drew sweat from Alan but not yet blood.

Effie to the rescue! "Alan," I said, disguising my voice, "could I speak to you a moment privately?"

He got up and followed me into the kitchen. A wind had sprung up and the screen door started to bang. Alan hooked it in place. "I found a little can of green paint in your garage," I said. "Same color as the car."

"Really?" He looked genuinely surprised. "Paint? Oh, I know. They gave it to me when I had the Porsche repainted, so if I got any dings I could touch it up. I'd forgotten all about it. I swear. Jane, you've got to believe me. God, what a mess. And that woman! I can't believe Mom duped her and she thinks I wrote all the pages. Of course, they really are my pages—essentially. Still . . . I feel guilty about it and that makes me look like I feel guilty about the accident. Frankly, she scares the shit out of me. Get me out of here. Do you have a car?"

"No, I walked."

"When did you learn to drive, by the way?"

"Last summer. Gled taught me."

"This fucking Gled has become a total force in my life. He's keeping me from my millions and teaching my wife things I should teach her."

"You never cared," I reminded him. "And it was Danny who taught me to swim."

"But I didn't think you wanted to know those things. You were always reading, writing, doing T'ai Chi, or trying to drink. I did want to teach you tennis, but you wanted to play pool instead. And didn't I offer to take you sailing? I'm not such a bad guy. Except for the abortion . . ." He looked hangdog. I hated to see him hangdog. He was still quite fragile. "Let's never mention the abortion again," I said. "I understood at the time and I've forgiven you long ago. Everything turned out fine."

"Where's Corinne? I want to see her."

"At the quarry."

"Gled's place, right? Show me the way. I'm going to get her." Hangdog became history and arrogant modern times. That's okay, arrogant suited him. I was comfortable with arrogant.

"No. Stick to the shore. Go talk to your agent. Tell her you want to vomit. Don't sign the contract."

Storm clouds were gathering as I hurried along High Street. Milk was gathering too, hurting my breasts. The blustery wind blew my hair around, making it even more raggedy, and as I entered the quarry driveway, big drops began to splatter down, making rings in the quarry water while thunder gnawed at the edges of the sky.

I wasn't thinking very straight or I'd have realized that Janice would naturally be coming to the quarry—the summer home she shared with Gled but she paid the taxes on—and then all would be revealed to her.

Sure enough, an hour later she walked in and found me

sitting in the bay window overlooking the quarry, watching the rain course down, nursing Corinne. There was a crack of thunder. The lights blinked and a branch of lightning clawed at the sky.

"Effie?" she said. "Is it you?"

{23} Swan Dive

She sat down opposite me and there was a long silence. Janice was at a loss. She didn't know what to say or think or do. She just stared at me. I had the strangest feeling of being the one in control. The worst had happened. Janice, of all people, had discovered my bigamy and yet I wasn't scared. I was calm. Maybe because she was so unnerved. If she'd gotten all villainous and rubbed her hands and said, "Ah-ha!" I might have been scared.

"Please don't say anything until I'm through nursing Corinne. I like this to be a peaceful time for her." (And me.)

She stared as if she'd never seen a nursing mother before. Maybe she hadn't.

The rain poured down. Mom was in the kitchen with Mrs. Flanagan. I could hear the murmur of their voices, the sound of dishes, the refrigerator door.

Janice got up and went to the piano where Gled was wont to pound out his Souza marches. She played some classical piece whose composer I didn't know. I didn't know any composers. Big gap in my education. Anyhow, it was lovely, beautifully rendered, and I was surprised that a bitch could make such beautiful music. No one is entirely what they seem.

She kept playing. I carried Corinne into the kitchen. Mrs. Flanagan and my mom could delight in her while I talked to Janice. On the way back to the living room, I shook myself out of the dreamy nursing mode and sharpened my wits.

Janice finished the piece and stood up. She was very tall. She loomed over me. Her teeth flashed. I put on lamps to illuminate the storm-darkened room and moved away from the window to the couch by the fire, which was out.

I decided I wouldn't say anything. Why should I? It was none of her business. But she beat me to it, announcing my decision before I did.

"You don't have to explain anything to me, Effie," she said, sitting down across from me. "The story is self-evident. You were married to Alan. You left him when he wanted you to abort the child, then went to California to have the baby, and when you heard about Danny, you married Gled out of sympathy. The only trouble is: You neglected to divorce Alan first. You probably would never have come back, but Alan needed you and you came. All this only makes you a nice person. Who am I to judge?"

Last summer she'd felt wholly qualified to judge me. Why this big change? Well, in fact she just did judge me and found me to be a nice person. If Janice judged me as nice, I had to rethink nice and see if it was something I wanted to be. Last summer I was a manipulative, greedy, little fortune hunter. Did being plump make the difference, make me nice? I didn't trust her for a second.

"I won't say anything to Gled," she said. "Or Martha."

I didn't believe her. She wanted something.

She didn't waste time letting me know what. "Both your mother and Martha tell me you're investigating the hit-and-run. I want you to drop it. Gled has finally come around to letting it go, now that Danny's recovering, and I don't believe for a minute Alan was involved."

She wanted the contracts signed. I was preventing Alan from signing the contracts. That was it.

The rain squall doubled its intensity, hitting the roof with dump-truck force. Thunder and lightning disturbed the room and a loud crack reverberated from the yard. I jumped as a tree branch sailed by the window.

Janice paid no attention. She was focused on me. "Effie, do you think Alan was the hit-and-run driver?"

"No."

The mini-paint can appeared in my mind's eye like a Warhol painting.

"Then what's the problem?"

"I feel that his name should be cleared. It's a black cloud over his head. What if everyone in the village thinks he did it?"

She lit a cigarette with a gold lighter and took a deep drag. "Then he can fucking well move away. He's a millionaire."

"True."

"And you can go with him or move back West, whatever you want."

"Right now I want to stay here. Gled's coming and I'm trying to persuade Lynn to let us have Danny for a while. Gled desperately needs some time with Danny in his own house."

"She'll never let you have him in a million years. Anyhow, all I'm asking now is for you to drop the investigation. You'll only stir things up for poor Gled."

She wanted the contracts signed before the publisher got wind of the . . . the what? *Scandal* was too mild a word.

"It will be the best thing for Gled too. He's obsessed. Whenever he's here, he spends hours at the site of the accident, then goes around town talking to everyone about it, just like you did today. I came here before going to see Martha and Alan and your mother told me what you were up to."

"I've got to think about this," I said.

"Don't let me stop you. I'm going for a swim in the quarry."

"In a thunderstorm?"

"I need my cheap thrills when I'm out of New York. Too much peace and beauty gets on my nerves. I love thunderstorms."

Another thunderous peal and the lights went off. It still wasn't night, but Mrs. Flanagan came into the room with candles and kerosene lamps. Mr. Flanagan carried in wood, then set the fire and lit it. It was a masterful job. Mom brought Corinne and settled in front of the fire.

I was back at the bay window. Soon I saw Janice on the cliff from which I'd stepped backward into the quarry last summer. She was naked. She did a swan dive into the quarry, as if showing the enormous difference between us. She was a woman without fear. If she'd been trapped in that rustic rest room, she'd have got out her gold lighter, burned it down around her, then stepped out free and clear, pausing only to urinate, standing up, on a last dying ember.

I got the old *Birds of America* book and, sitting down by Mom, looked up swans.

I read aloud about them to Corinne while she waved her arms and kicked her legs. " 'The swans are famous for their stately appearance in the water,' " I told her, " 'due largely to the constantly changing but always graceful arching of their necks.' "

"Hi, Lynn. It's Effie again. Look, I've got a great idea. Why don't you bring Danny to the quarry and stay here with us? That way you won't worry about him and it would be nice for Danny to see us all together. Janice is here too."

"Ugh!"

"Maybe she's going tomorrow. I'll make her go if you want me to. What do you say? Will you come?"

"I would like to spend time at the quarry again. I love that place. Maybe it would work. Danny seems awfully unhappy. Maybe it would cheer him up."

"Great! I'll get a message to Gled and he can pick you up on the way from the airport. He'll be so happy."

"Why don't you give me his flight number and we'll pick him up?"

"That's even better. Lynn, you're the best. I'm so grateful."

Mom was already in bed when I came to her room. She was reading. I crawled in beside her and snuggled my head on her shoulder. She kissed my brow. I loved the mom smell of her. "Janice knows," I told her.

"Oh, Effie. You're in big trouble now."

She put aside her book and sat up, plumping the pillow behind her. She reached for her knitting, but there was no knitting.

"She says she's not going to tell Gled or Martha."

"Not going to tell the brother she adores? Why?"

"I'm not entirely sure. She says she wants me to stop looking into the hit-and-run. She thinks I'm keeping Alan from signing the contracts until it's cleared up. Which I am."

Mom sighed. "All the more reason to get it cleared up, it seems to me."

"Maybe Janice thinks he did it and wants the contracts signed before it comes out."

"Okay, but meanwhile, why isn't she telling Gled you're a bigamist?"

"Maybe she wants to keep on my good side until the contracts are signed."

"Effie, honey." Her fingers made knitting motions. "I think your days are numbered. I wish I'd brought wool."

I was falling asleep. I slid out of the bed. "I'm going to sleep here, okay? I'll go get Corinne. Oh and guess what? Tomorrow Lynn and Danny are coming, along with Gled. I can't wait to see Danny."

"What about Gled, your husband? Are you excited to see him?" Mom asked when Corinne and I got into bed beside her.

"It totally pales next to the excitement of seeing Danny. Here we are, Mom, three generations. Read us to sleep, okay?"

"But, honey, what are you going to do?"

"I'm going to find out who hit Danny and then, I guess, I'm going to tell my husbands I'm a bigamist."

"Good. Much better they find out from you than Janice. And I worry about the girls letting something slip. They're wonderful, but, well, I've never liked to say this, but they're not as smart as you are Effie."

"Who, the women? Wrong, Mom, they're way smarter than I am."

{24} Kicks

The prettiest, most balletic parts of the form are the kicks called Separate the Right Foot, followed by Separate the Left Foot. At the same time, you are separating your arms and hands from an arc formed in front of you. You are striking with your toes, so they are pointed. From these kicks you Turn Around and Strike with Heel, which is not so pretty and is a difficult balancing act, being a much higher kick than the others, out to the side. It is the dramatic kick found in all martial arts and shown on posters. Then after Riding the Tiger comes the Lotus Kick, which is a kick straight ahead, only with a circular movement thrown in. With all these kicks, it is important to focus your eyes in the direction you are kicking. In every move, the eyes are in line with the navel, so all three are moving and gazing in concert. Behind the navel is the seat of the *tan t'ien:* power, balance, sinking, rooting, energy.

Above all, the mind is focused. T'ai Chi is the martial art of the mind.

My mind had never been so focused as it was the day Gled, Lynn, and Danny arrived at the quarry, where I, Corinne, my mom and Janice were already ensconced. Somehow I knew that this was the day all of our lives would be resolved. Mine particularly needed resolution. Corinne's life was too new to need resolution but depended a lot on my getting my life straight. From now on, whatever I did in my life affected hers. I had to think for two. (First you eat for two, then you think for two, then you keep on eating for two.)

To achieve resolution, I had to be resolute, tenacious, decisive. I couldn't let Alan or Janice push me around—they being the main two who liked to get their way—or to get their millions, as it were.

Last night, before sleep, Mom and I had kept talking about the bigamy angle. She made a joke. "It was all my fault. You made me so happy marrying Alan that you probably thought you'd make me twice as happy marrying Gled too."

"That's right. I wanted to give you two beautiful summer houses instead of one."

"A boon to a lifelong city apartment dweller like me. But, Effie, as you'll find out, all a mother wants is her own child's happiness, but—here's the rub—she shouldn't be the one to determine what that happiness is. I've been doing a lot of thinking. You, being the oldest, took on the burden of succeeding. You've pushed yourself ever since you were small. You've always worked. And you've studied so hard. Then you married, taking on another burden when you already had your thesis to write. I think it was almost a given that you would have a physical, moral, and intellectual collapse—giving up everything, throwing it all away. But out of it all came Corinne, so we're winners."

"Right. And don't be surprised if I stay collapsed."

"Nothing you do will ever surprise me after this." She sighed heavily.

Gled, Danny, and Lynn arrived around noon. The storm had left the air clear and fresh. The sky was blue without a scrap of cloud but sometimes scraps of birds. Wildflowers had opened all over the yard, as if a fairy gardener had come and planted in the night. The quarry was like a mirror and the surrounding trees were all duplicated upside down, the green foliage as if plunged into the pale blue water. Along with the rocks and trees, I imagined the swan dive reflected there too for all eternity, layered over my backward tumble from the same cliff.

I went to meet them and Gled jumped from the car to run and meet me, making me feel a little embarrassed because of Lynn, but also feeling warm and happy to be so ardently embraced by him. I always felt a little surprised to discover and rediscover that my employer really loved me and thought I was wonderful.

Lynn, who I half-feared would be an older replica of me because of the way men are or—worse fear—a younger replica of Janice, had her own look: medium height, beautiful long dark hair, half-Asian or maybe American Indian, which I hadn't known, serious-looking, which could be due to her current strain.

Danny didn't look too bad. Like his dad, he was a lot thinner and somehow not as curly-haired. He was subdued but did not seem unhappy.

Lynn was sweet about Corinne, making much of her little irresistible self, but Gled, as usual, resisted, not quite giving her the cold shoulder, but almost. Danny right away wanted to hold her. I knew he would because, after all, he's the best little boy in the world, never mind that he didn't remember he was or remember who any of us were. The great thing about Corinne was that he didn't need to remember her. She hadn't been around. They were starting out together.

"Look," he said. "She's smiling." She was. She was smiling at Danny.

"My little sister," he said, proud and full of wonder. Suddenly Gled looked at Corinne the same way as Danny—really seeing her, acknowledging her at last. Smiling, he bent over her where she lay in Danny's arms and tenderly stroked her cheek. Tears came to my eyes. My new family, at last, was all together.

Later in the day, I found everyone up at the tennis court where Janice and Gled were going at it tooth and nail but joking and laughing too. "I don't remember how to play," Danny said happily and I remembered how he'd never liked his lessons. Amnesia could be useful.

Lynn was sitting within touching distance of Danny. They were drinking lemonade and watching the game.

I was going to ask her if I could take him for a ride, but then I thought it would be better just to inform her. "Lynn, I'm going to take Danny to Lanes Cove. We had a wonderful day together there last summer and I have this feeling that if we go again it might help his memory."

Danny chugged his lemonade and stood up, ready for action.

"I don't think so," Lynn said.

"C'mon, Mom. I'm sick of sitting here doing nothing. You won't let me swim. You . . ."

"Please, Lynn. It will be good for Danny."

"I'll go with you, then." She stood up tensely.

"I was his nanny, remember? He's in good hands. I'm his stepmother too."

The tennis players were missing balls, looking over at us. I hoped they would keep out of it. "Come on, Danny." I started off and he followed. Lynn followed too.

"I can't allow this," Lynn said. "Danny is simply not up to walking any distance."

I remembered how Danny had been in perpetual motion that summer day, sailing along on his skateboard with balance, grace, and confidence—leaping, twisting, flying.

We were passing Gled, who was bouncing the ball, preparing to serve.

"Take the convertible," he called cheerily. "The top's down. The key is in the ignition."

"Do you see how he just leaves the key in for anyone to steal . . ." Lynn cried.

We walked down the steps from the court and past the quarry. "Lynn, I'm taking Danny by myself. We'll be back in an hour. Please don't worry."

She started to cry and wring her hands. Danny hung his head and kicked the ground. "I beg of you," she began.

"Danny, get in the car, okay? I'll be right there."

He looked indecisively at his mother. "Go on," I told him. I took Lynn in my arms and she cried and whimpered. "I'm just so tired," she said. "I feel so helpless. I can't go on. It's too hard."

"The worst is over, Lynn. Things can only get better now. What you've got to remember about Danny is that he's a totally together little boy who knows just what he's doing. He's smart, athletic, and coordinated and doesn't take any chances. What happened was not his fault and it certainly wasn't Gled's fault. It was the fault of the son of a bitch who came too fast around the curve and hit him."

"I can't go on."

"Yes, you can. You're probably sleep-deprived." That was the least of it, but it would make her feel better to give it a name that wasn't *nervous breakdown.* "Go inside and take a nap. We'll be back in an hour. I promise." I pushed her toward the house.

"If you get out of the car, hold his hand . . ."

She called a stream of instructions to me, but I was in the car and out of hearing before she'd got halfway.

I tried not to look as glum as I felt, but all I could think was how it just wasn't good for Danny to be living alone with his scared mother. He needed his daredevil father too. And so did she. "The women" were right. It was too much strain on her, handling this tragedy alone. And her refusing to let Gled participate in Danny's care gave her no reprieve.

I parked in the village. We bought two Popsicles, then

walked slowly down to the cove. We weren't chattering away as we'd always done before, but that was okay. The silence was comfortable. Danny looked around.

There were two artists painting the picturesque breakwater, their easels set close together so they could talk.

A lobsterman was tying his dory up to the quay and unloading a basket of lobsters. We looked at the strange green crustaceans all piled on top of one another. Danny, laughing, picked one up and watched it flail its claws and flap its tail. I hoped he wouldn't get bitten or I'd have to commit *hara-kiri* in front of Lynn.

We walked out on the breakwater and sat down, looking back into the cove. It wasn't as hot as it had been the other day we'd come.

Danny asked me about the gulls: how you could tell a female from a male, a young gull from an adult. It was a little like he was being polite, getting me to talk about what he knew interested me, since he himself didn't have any interests.

I obliged and rambled happily on. He seemed to be only half-listening. I wished I had a Sylvester Stallone movie to tell him about so I could be more amusing. He didn't notice when I stopped talking. He was thinking.

Finally he said, "Gulls aren't much compared to hummingbirds."

My breath caught in my throat. Tears jumped to my eyes. He turned to me, his eyes big. "Remember, Effie, how they flew all those miles, their wings . . . their wings beating so fast!"

"Ninety beats a minute," I shouted and hugged him. "Oh Danny, Danny!"

"They can fly upside down!" he said. "They can hover!"

"Yes! Yes! And they can cling . . ."

"And perch . . ."

"But they can't walk!" we shouted together.

We got up and held hands and danced around in a circle. "I'm remembering, aren't I, Effie?"

"Yes, it's coming back. Your memory's coming back."

"And then I taught you to swim. Didn't I teach you to swim that day?"

"You sure did."

"You kept sinking. It took me hours. You were pathetic."

"You are really something, Danny. Let's go home and tell everyone the good news."

"I still don't remember everything," he said in the car.

"Never mind. It's coming. It's like a little leak through a pinhole and then, as the water comes through, the hole gets bigger and bigger until it breaks apart the whole fucking levee! Excuse me."

Danny laughed hilariously at the bad word.

"Your memories are trickling now, but pretty soon they'll be gushing. You'll see."

On the way to the quarry, as we approached the driveway, an old man was walking along very slowly. Talk about memory. I'd completely forgotten Walker Hancock. How could I? That great man. Another of my happiest days! Gone from my mind. Why? Maybe because I hadn't walked his property since my return. There's something about the actual putting of your feet on the ground where it happened that presses a memory to the fore. I'm sure with Danny it was being on the granite breakwater that did it.

I stopped the car. "Hello, Mr. Hancock," I said. As usual, he looked freshly groomed, almost debonair.

"Hello, Effie. Why, Danny, it's you. How are you doing, son?"

"Fine. I just started to remember some things today. Down in Lanes Cove."

"That's wonderful. Well, we're all pulling for you."

"I can't wait to tell my mom and dad."

"I'm going to leave Danny off at home and then I want to come back and talk to you, Mr. Hancock. Please keep on with your walk," I told him, "and I'll catch up."

Honking, I dropped Danny, watched as Mrs. Flanagan met him, then started back on foot to the end of the drive. Overhead the leaves started to rustle to the tune of a wind off the sea. Mr. Hancock hadn't gotten much farther and soon I was beside him.

After making small talk, I said, "I wanted to ask you about the day of the accident. Possibly you were out walking on High Street as usual."

"Yes, I was. But I never go that far down. The community garden is my turnaround point. Janice found him, you know. I saw Janice go by."

"You did?"

"Yes. She was going fast. Too fast, I thought at the time. She looked mad, but she almost always looks sort of mad, poor child."

I guess when you're in your nineties, everyone else is a child.

"She was mad because she'd told Danny not to go skateboarding and he disobeyed her," I told Walker.

"Well, kids . . ." he trailed off.

We walked a little farther. I was thinking hard, feeling scared. "Walker, you're so visual," I said tentatively. "Maybe you remember what color car Janice was driving. It was a rent-a-car, probably a Ford or Mercury."

"Yes, I can. It was green."

"There was green paint on the skateboard."

"I heard."

"Walker . . . what if it were Janice herself who hit him?"

"Poor child," he said—and he could have meant either Danny or Janice. "What a tragedy."

My mind reeled. I spoke rapidly. "She was driving fast and she was mad. It's not a good combination. She could have come around that curve and hit him. No one was around. She called the ambulance on her cell phone and then just said she'd found him on the road. She would have found it impossible to tell Gled the truth."

Then later, I thought to myself, she tries to buy him a new child. When I come back and start looking into it, she tries to stop me. She says she won't tell Gled about my bigamy because that gives her a hold over me in case I happen on the truth.

"I thought at the time that it had to be her," he said. "But it wasn't my business. I didn't interfere. It was all in the family. She and Gled lost their parents young, you know. All they had was each other. They're awfully close."

"Do you think the village knows it's her?"

"I wouldn't be surprised. Who would leave a child on the road? It's unimaginable. This way nobody did."

That's why no one could help Gled as he went around like the Ancient Mariner, clutching at people's sleeves, asking for intelligence to illuminate the accident. They didn't dare say what they were thinking.

Now that I knew, it seemed so obvious. But even if the suspicion had occurred to Gled, he'd ignore it, never believing that Janice would stay mute.

Twenty minutes later, I found Janice alone in the little-used backyard of the quarry house, sort of a glade. She was sitting in an Adirondack chair, reading a manuscript. A glass of iced tea was on the arm of the chair. There were typewritten pages in her hand and the rest of the manuscript was under a rock to preserve it from the breezes.

In back of her was a lily pond that Mr. Flanagan had established, with a lovely, old, life-sized stone statue of a woman perched in a shady hollow above it. There were ferns around the statue along with some last lilies of the valley. Spring endured longer in the shade.

"I've found out," I said solemnly. "You were the one who hit Danny."

She flushed and tossed aside the pages. She leapt from the chair, grabbing up the rock, and ran at me full speed, the rock-holding hand raised to deliver a blow. I could have unleashed one of my kicks, but I didn't. It would have been overreacting and, anyhow, I wasn't prepared for her getting physical. I was barely prepared enough to step aside, to vanish. She wheeled and came after me again. I was calm but not so calm I didn't feel as if someone else were behind me. I glanced back to see the stone lady and, at that moment, Janice grabbed me by one shoulder and got set to bash me in the head with the rock. With T'ai Chi pliability, I wriggled away like a fish and got to the other side of the big wooden chair. I couldn't shake the feeling that the stone statue was on Janice's side, her backup. It wasn't fair. Two against one.

"Let's talk about it," I said. "Calm down."

We were circling the chair, sometimes reversing directions the way little kids do when one is trying to get the other. This was not good T'ai Chi. Janice was saying words but not "talking about it." Instead, she was providing a description of her feelings about me, embroidered with an impressive vocabulary of obscenities. I couldn't think how to invoke my martial art in a useful way, so I simply made a break for it, clambered up the bank, and got behind the stone lady so that I could stop worrying about her sneaking up on me from the rear. The rock went whizzing by my head just as I stepped behind her.

Janice came after me, lost her footing, and fell into the lily pond. I'd like to think it was the power of my mind that did it. I believe it was. Or maybe it was the power of the stone lady's mind. Oh hell, she just slipped. And a good thing too. She probably would have killed me, called an ambulance on her cell phone, and told everyone she just found me there with my head battered in. Rock-and-run.

Something about the ignominy of her position, sitting in the shallow pond, adrape with lily pads, made her lose heart. Her lower lip began to tremble.

"It's not true," she lied. "It's not true."

"It's true, Janice, but Gled will forgive you. You've got to tell him." I gave her a hand out of the pond. She was scraped and bleeding but just superficially, as opposed to how my head would have looked had all gone as she had hoped.

"I'll tell him about *you.* That's what I'll tell him."

"Danny's okay now. He started to recover his memory today. He's going to be fine. It was an accident. But Gled has to know. And you have to unburden yourself. You can't live with this secret. It will tear you up."

She sat down on the chair. Her mouth still trembled. "You can't know what I've suffered."

I could imagine, but I didn't care. Suffering would do her good. The more the better. Although probably she had only feared discovery and thought *that* was suffering.

"My entire life changed in that instant of collision."

I sat down on the grass, all attention. She fumbled in a straw bag by her chair, brought out a small silver flask, and poured the contents into her ice tea. Manuscript pages littered the glade.

"One minute I had the world by the tail and the next minute I was the murderer of my brother's son. Life would never be the same. Never. If he found out, the man I loved most in the world—the only person I ever loved—would hate me. If I could have changed places with Danny, I would have. I wished with all my heart it were me lying bloody on the road, not him."

I didn't want to credit her with feelings, but I began to think she had suffered. I believed in her love for Gled. That was a constant and central to her life. Yes, that must have been a bad moment, seeing Danny on the road—and the ensuing months must have been pretty horrible too, as he hovered between life and death.

"Not a night goes by that I don't wake up and relive that moment."

Still, all of the above being the case, why was she so quick to try and bloody me? Would she have awakened every night and relived that moment, too? I suppose, when she grabbed that rock, she was scared and wasn't thinking. But she was angry and wasn't thinking when she ran down Danny.

"Everything's okay now, Janice. Tell him. It won't be easy but you'll be glad."

"I'll never tell him and if you do I'll deny it until my dying breath. I'm leaving the country tonight."

"The village knows." I said, standing up. It sounded ominous. It was worse than saying "God knows" because the village really exists. I spoke on.

"You've got to get a leash on your anger and you've got to give up having to be in control of everyone around you. All this begins with telling Gled. It's not even what you did to Danny that worries you; it's that you can't bear to have Gled see you so flawed, his perfect brilliant older sister, the great success story, the taxpayer.

"I'm going to tell Gled about Alan. That's not going to be easy either, to display myself as a criminal and a fool, but that's how life is, right? There's this great artist, Bea Wood, she's almost a hundred years old, and she says, 'It's the hardships of life that teach you to overcome the hardships of life.' "

"Oh, shut up! You just go your merry way. You don't know what hardship is."

I could have told her about being trapped in the National Park rest room when my water broke, but the hell with it. Other people's hardships never seem as bad as theirs and, really, I had to admit, hers took the cake, making my hardship pretty piddling. I'd tell her another time.

I turned and left the glade, walking slowly, going my merry

way, not looking back, even though there was a feeling at the back of my neck that a rock could come winging my way because I knew her dreadful secret and because I didn't know what hardship was.

The others were all out front, sitting on the white wrought-iron furniture under the maple tree. "Gled, can I please talk to you for a minute alone?"

Alone in my bedroom, Gled embraced me. Right away I felt sexy. We hadn't made love except for the one time on our wedding night because of the baby and his being away. All in all, I'd had much less sex with two husbands that I'd had with one, so I don't think bigamy is for everyone.

"Effie," he said joyfully, "you're a miracle worker. Danny's remembering. I think he knows me now. Life is beginning for me. I'd lost all hope, Effie, and I just couldn't seem to get it back. I know the true meaning of the word *hopeless* and I wouldn't wish it on anyone. God, how I've suffered. Thank God I've survived to see this day. There were times when I thought about letting my airplane fall out of the sky, but I was too afraid of hitting someone below."

"Gled, this will sound strange, coming from me, but I think you should get back together with Lynn. Danny needs you both and he needs you together. He desperately needs your courage in an ongoing way. All three of you still need a lot of healing and the best way is to be together."

"Effie, I think so too. I've been thinking of nothing else and I think Lynn would have me. I think she needs me."

I wished he hadn't been quite so quick to agree, because as soon as he did, I felt sad and hurt. I wished he'd at least had a small agony of indecision. I felt heartbroken and unloved. But it was what I wanted for Danny and, being a bigamist, I was in no position to complain when Gled agreed it was for the best.

"I think all this has been terribly hard on Lynn," he continued. "She's not doing well. There are times when she doesn't even make sense. I think she held herself together all through the coma, but now she's falling apart. And what Danny needs most is strength and normalcy around him. But what about you?" At last he looked at me with concern, even anguish. "I'd feel like a rat to leave you with your—our—newborn baby. And it's you I love, Effie, not Lynn. What shall I do?"

I took a moment to savor the emotion, then launched my confession.

"Gled, our marriage isn't any good. I'm married to someone else: Alan Croy."

He frowned terribly, but it was at Alan's name, not at my admission. "The man who might have hit Danny?"

"He didn't do it. He's been completely exonerated."

"I'm sorry I accused him. But, Effie, you don't want to be married to a man like that."

"That's right, I don't. That's why I left him."

"Was he the one you came back to see?"

"Yes. He was feeling so bad about everything—me, the baby he'd asked me to lose, being accused of the hit-and-run—that he tried to kill himself."

"So now you love him again and want to be with him?"

"No. Not more than you, Gled. The one I love most is Danny and I want what's best for him."

"You are wonderful."

"I know."

"Poor Effie, you've suffered too." Again he took me in his arms and again I felt sexy because of his body against mine and because of his understanding.

"Being trapped in the rest room was terrible," I said.

"It certainly was," he agreed, holding me close. We both started to laugh. The laughter vibrated our closely held bodies.

"My shoulder will never be the same from trying to open that door. You should really have a License to Push, Effie, going around with that secret weapon. It's not safe for the community at large."

We held each other tighter and our bodies grew aroused even as we laughed and talked. "I'll have my lawyer take care of the bigamy. He'll know what to do, probably just dissolve the second marriage. But always think of me as a husband, Effie. I love you."

"I'm thinking of you as a husband right now."

We made love. I have to take these hardships as they come and go my merry way.

He was a first-class lover. He didn't spare himself. He touched me and kissed me and sang my praises. He was with me all the way, keenly attentive until he lost himself in his orgasm, but even then he took me with him. With Gled, there was no feeling of being alone. The height of intimacy that consummation was supposed to be, with Gled, really was the height of intimacy, a tender joining, losing boundaries, not knowing who was who.

"You're a blue-ribbon lover," I said after we'd showered and were getting dressed.

"We should be together, Effie."

"I know. But Danny . . . and Lynn. The worst is over, but it's when the worst is over that you sometimes fall to pieces. She can't hack it alone. Ellie and Edna were the first to make me realize that."

He frowned. "Effie, I don't know if I'll be able to provide for you and Corinne. I'll do what I can."

"Don't worry about it. I'm the mistress of getting by."

"I will worry about it. She's Danny's little sister." He was watching me in the mirror where he was combing his hair. "Will you stay here in the East?"

"I'm going back to California. I'm going to try to get Emma, Ellie, and Edna to come with me." Why not Elma too? I thought and giggled. "But first I have to tell Alan. I'll go see him after dinner."

"Are you going to sleep with Alan too?" Gled asked jealously.

"What kind of woman do you think I am?"

The telephone rang.

"Gled speaking."

"This is Alan Croy. I want you to know I've been absolved of the hit-and-run of your son. Janice has informed me that the real perpetrator is known."

"Janice? Why didn't she inform me?"

"She was anxious to have me sign a contract, which I wouldn't do until I felt cleared of the crime. As soon as she found out, she came over."

"Who was it?"

"She can't say. But I have to get Jane's okay before signing. Is she there?"

"Jane?"

"My wife."

"Right. Hold on."

"Hi, Alan, I was about to call. What's up?"

"Janice has discovered the hit-and-run driver and says I'm completely cleared. Still, I didn't want to sign without your approval and, for all I know, she's pulling a fast one."

"No, she's right. We both know who it is and it isn't you."

"What a relief."

"Alan, I'm coming over after dinner. I have to talk to you."

"Bring Corinne."

When I hung up the phone, Gled said, "Jane?"

"Middle name. I got rid of 'Effie,' then took it back the day I left Alan and met you."

"Sometime I have to hear the whole story, but first . . . I just heard you tell Alan that both you and Janice know who hit Danny."

"I can't say who it was, Gled."

He grabbed my shoulders as Janice had earlier. Again I became fish and wriggled away. Luckily, the stone lady wasn't anywhere around. "Please, just ask Janice."

"Did she find out from the auto-body shop investigation?"

I wanted to say that the investigation wasn't going anywhere since Hertz had their own body shops.

"I think I hear Corinne crying," I said and made good my escape.

"Corinne never cries!" he called after me.

{25} Step Forward to the Seven Stars of the Dipper

After the second Snake Creeps Down, you rise up, shift your weight to your left foot, take a half-step forward with your right foot, toe touching the ground, while you form both hands into fists and join them at the wrists in front of your chest.

Stepping Up to the Stars, to me, always signals the approach of the end of the form.

I thought of this before going to see Alan. I was coming to the end and he was the star I was stepping up to.

It was too bad he'd signed the contracts before my confession. He'd be much less understanding. A golden-haired writer with two million dollars is different from an assistant professor pulling down forty thousand a year before taxes.

"Effie, what are you going to do?" Mom asked as we packed up our things together. This had become an oft-repeated query with her, usually accompanied by a sigh, although I'd asked her not to sigh in front of Corinne.

"Whatever happens with Alan, we're leaving the quarry today." I told her about my wanting Danny to be with his parents and how Gled thought so too.

"You're right. It's the best thing. It's awfully sad, though, for you and Gled."

"Children are more important than grown-ups, don't you think?"

"You have to look out for yourself, Effie."

"But see, I've got you, Mom. I always know you're there for me, no matter what. Who does Danny have? Who can he count on?"

I gave her woebegone face a big kiss. "You finish packing and load the car so we'll be ready to go when I come back."

"Maybe Alan will beg you to stay with him."

"Why do I feel that will never happen? He's not a forgiver, Mom."

I borrowed the Toyota. Janice was emerging from the shore road as I stopped at the end of High Street preparatory to crossing over, but she turned right, leaving town, probably heading for the airport, going off without telling Gled about Danny.

Martha and Alan were at the dining room table eating lobster and drinking champagne by candlelight.

As promised, I'd brought Corinne, and after Alan had held her and fussed over her, praised her beauty and intelligence, Martha took her on her lap while I sat down to a butter-laden leftover lobster tail, after which I sucked away at some of the tiny legs attached to the body that no one else ever bothered with. I figured a glass of champagne wouldn't hurt either—my first drink in ten months. It was fantastic. Luckily, it was the end of the bottle or I'd have kept on sipping and sucking and forgone the confession entirely.

Alan was lauding Janice, not only as a consummate dealmaker but as Lanesville's answer to Sherlock Holmes, having discovered the hit-and-run artist. I let it go. Let him think what he wanted.

"So," he said, winding down on the Janice paean, "did you come to celebrate or is there something on your mind?"

"Any more champagne?"

"No, sorry."

"Let's go out on the porch a minute."

It was too dark and windy on the porch, so we came back in. Martha had taken Corinne to the living room. The dining room and kitchen were too messy to talk in and I didn't want to have it out in Alan's bedroom or any bedroom. Maybe the champagne had befuddled me, but I couldn't for the life of me think where to go to tell Alan I was a bigamist. Certainly not the garage. And I didn't want to go to the attic—where the mice were.

"Jane, will you settle down? What's the matter with you?" Alan was trailing after me as we went hither and thither.

There was a cedar chest in the upstairs hall. We could sit on the cedar chest. I trotted up the stairs, Alan close behind, his face falling a bit when I bypassed his bedroom door. I sat down on the chest, patting the place beside me, and he sat down too. It was sort of like sitting on a bench waiting for the bus to come.

"Alan, when I was in San Francisco, I married Gled Saltonstall."

"You what?" He jumped up from the chest. "Surely he knew you were married to me?"

"No. I never told him."

"When you were working for him, you said you were single? Why?"

"I'd left you when I went to work for him. When things changed and we were back together, I . . ."

"But why on earth would he marry a pregnant woman?" Alan exclaimed, leaping ahead.

"He thought the baby could be his child."

"This is unbelievable." Alan paced back and forth in front of me. He clasped his brow and it was a heartfelt gesture, not a pose. I felt uncomfortable. This wasn't easy. I felt like clasping my own brow.

The hall space was cramped and not very paceable because

of the stairwell. He stopped and stared at me. "Wait a minute . . ."

"Alan, if you'd just let me tell you instead of firing questions at me . . ."

"Is Corinne his child?"

"I don't know."

"That means you were lovers last summer. Good God! You . . ."

Take the cake? No, that was much too mild.

". . . slut!"

"I . . ." I stammered.

"While you were lovers with me. On our honeymoon! So!" He raised his voice over mine and I gave up trying to speak. "That means, when you told me you were pregnant with Corinne . . ." He raised his finger, making a point, the incipient millions not yet eliminating this academic trait. "I took on all the guilt of telling you to get an abortion when it wasn't even my child!"

"I would have told you then, but . . ."

"Do you know what I've suffered? I thought I was a murderer all these months and then almost killed myself, and all the while it wasn't even my baby! You are evil, Jane, evil."

I was an evil slut. No, Mom, I don't think Alan will beg me to stay.

I was sick of everyone telling me how they'd suffered. What about me?

"I've suffered too."

"Oh, really?" He looked as disbelieving as one can look while also looking hateful.

"Yes. You know how I've always been so afraid of public rest rooms . . ."

"Jane, this is not a joke."

"I'm not joking. I was in this rustic rest room in a National Park three thousand miles from home . . ."

"I don't give a shit. I don't want to hear about you having some stupid panic attack. We're talking about larger emotional matters here."

"I call terror and pain larger emotions, but probably they don't count as such because *you* haven't experienced them." I was going to tell this story, no matter what. "I was sealed in, at night, no lights, with labor coming on!"

"Labor is not an emotion. It's a process and you are hardly alone in having undergone it."

"Nor are you alone in *never having* to undergo it. For that matter, suicide is a process, although you *are* alone in having tried to vacuum yourself to death."

"That's enough now. You deceived me. You betrayed me. You became lovers with another man on our honeymoon! I almost lost my life . . ."

"What does it matter now? What matters is that Corinne is alive and you love her. She might be your daughter and she might not, but you love her just like I love Danny. The true parent is the loving parent."

"I don't love Corinne if she isn't my child. I loved her because I thought she was and because I was so happy she was alive."

"I don't understand. How can you stop loving an innocent baby that you loved a minute ago, just because she might not be yours?"

"No, you *don't* understand. You don't understand anything. You're hopeless. I want you out of my life. And don't try to get any money from me because there's no way you'll have the law on your side. What's Gled going to do? Have you told him? I suppose you did and he dropped you cold, so then you came to me."

"Alan, you're upset and I know you're going to feel bad about things you've said because you're essentially a good person. I came to tell you the truth and to tell you I'm going back to

California. I don't want anything from you, except your love for Corinne."

"Don't you feel any remorse at all?"

I thought about it. I examined my mind and heart. "No. I don't think so. I'm sorry about your suicide attempt, but I did come to your side at once and I do think it had to do with things other than me. I think it was being accused of the hit-and-run and I think a lot of it was being unable to write your novel and realizing that you were hot air."

"Get out of my house!"

Not only was his mother's novel his, her house was too. That's how it is with stars. Everything belongs to them, except their baby.

I did not go out the door. I went downstairs to the living room to take my sleeping baby from Martha.

"Darling," she said, "I didn't hear all of it, only the part where Alan shouted, but of course Corinne will always be family and I'll do everything I can to help financially."

"Thank you, Martha."

"I covered Corinne's ears when he shouted."

"You're wonderful."

"Mind you, the taxes on this house are deplorable, but I'll do what I can for both of you."

"We'll be all right."

"Maybe I should winterize it and give up my Boston apartment, but there's my season ticket to the symphony and there are no good restaurants on all of Cape Ann. I think I'd go mad here in the winter."

I kissed her. "We'll keep in touch. Come and see us in San Francisco."

"Take care, Jane. I . . . I . . . well, it's difficult to say and I'd hate for Alan to hear just now, feeling as he does—and with good reason—but . . . I love you. You're not an evil slut. You're good-hearted—to a fault."

"Thanks. I love you too."

"Do you want the rings? They're really yours."

"No. Keep them. Bye."

She called after me. "I'm dying to hear the whole rest room story."

"Bless you."

Back at the quarry, Mom was waiting for me with our bags packed in her car, an old Plymouth. "I'll just go say goodbye to Gled and Danny and Lynn."

I found them in the golden-paneled living room. They were all on the Chinese rug around a Monopoly board, looking like a happy family. I stood in the shadows, holding Corinne, sniffing her sweet-smelling downy head, feeling spurned, cast out. It was silly. It was Alan, not Gled, who had cast me out.

I felt sad and miserable. My heart hurt. I felt alone and unloved. Telling myself it was silly didn't help.

I wanted to slink away, but it would be rude and cowardly and Danny would be hurt. It wasn't fair to Corinne either, not to say goodbye to Danny.

Luckily, Danny looked up and saw us. "Effie, come play!"

I swallowed the lump in my throat and steeled myself. "I've come to say goodbye to you all. Mom and I are setting off."

I walked over and Danny got up and came to meet me halfway. "Off where? What about Dad?"

Had Gled not told him yet? Damn.

"Dad's staying with us, Danny," Lynn said. "We're all going to be together."

"Really, Effie?" asked Danny.

"Yes, honey, he wants you three to be a family again and that's what I want too."

"Really? He turned to his parents with a joyful grin. "Dad's going to live with us!" he said to his Mom. "Oh boy!"

Lynn got up and came over to me. "Thank you, Effie, for everything. You're a love."

"But I'll see Effie and Corinne, won't I?" Danny said. "She's my sister."

"Of course you will," I promised, wondering how.

"Goodbye, Corinne," he said, giving her a clumsy kiss. She grabbed his hair, tangling her fingers in his curls. "Ouch!" he said delightedly. "I'll get you for that." Corinne grinned.

Now the tears were coming. I had to get out of there. I turned, waving gaily. "Goodbye. I love you all." Once out of the living room, I ran through the house and out the door, over the lawn to the turnaround where Mom was parked. A crescent moon hung in the dappled sky, ready to catch something, maybe my tears.

"Effie, wait!"

Gled was beside me. "No, Gled, don't say anything. This is harder than I thought it would be."

"For me too. I don't know if I can do it. We never even had a chance to be together and when we were I was a zombie."

"Last summer you weren't. I'll remember you as you were last summer and as you were today."

"But I don't want to be remembered," he said, he who had wanted more than anything in the world to be remembered by his son. "I want to be present."

"It's Danny who needs you. And Lynn."

"And you don't?"

"I don't. I honestly don't." But I love you, I said to myself, wondering when I'd started loving him and when, if ever, it would end. Had it started when I fell off the cliff? Or was it starting right now?

He kissed me on the lips. He kissed Corinne on her cheek. She reached out her hand and cooed at him. He kissed her again. And me again. Then we said goodbye.

I cried a good deal of the way to Boston. Fortunately Mom didn't ask me or herself where she'd gone wrong.

"Janice? Gled speaking. I'm calling from San Francisco."

"Are you with Effie? I thought you'd gone back to Lynn."

"I have, but I'm keeping my job out here and keeping my apartment. I'll still mainly be on the East Coast, however. Why didn't you call me when you got back from Europe?"

"I've been jet-lagged."

"You never called me from Europe either. We've never been so out of touch."

"I . . . I'm sorry."

"I want to ask you something and I'm going to have to be blunt. Are you the one who hit Danny?"

"No."

"I can't seem to rest until I know. Just now, it came to me that it might have been you. It made sense. Everything fell into place."

"That little bitch told you, didn't she? She told you it was me?"

"Who, Lynn?"

"Not Lynn. I mean Effie. She's lying."

"Effie never told me any such thing."

"She didn't?"

"Back in June, the day you left, Alan told me both you and Effie knew who did it. Effie said to ask you. I figured you'd tell me, but you never did. You left the country. That got me thinking . . ."

"I didn't do it."

"If you did, I'd forgive you, Janice. Even if Danny had died, I'd forgive you. You're my sister. It was an appalling accident. It was not your fault. Are you there? Janice, are you crying?"

"Of course not. Agents don't cry."

"That's right. I forgot."

"Effie?"

"Hi, Danny. How are you, honey?"

"I feel a little kinda bored. I need you to tell me about a bird."

"Pigeons? All I see these days are pigeons."

"Try."

"There's the crane. The day I met you I was feeling like a crane. It's a great bird. And they're considered good luck in Japan and symbols of peace. Next time you're at the quarry, look on the wall by the bookcase. There's a neat picture of two cranes by Hiroshige, a Japanese artist who was born almost two hundred years ago. He was a fireman, like his father and like his son would be, but he wanted to be an artist. He left the fire department to study art, disappointing his father as I disappointed my mother. He traveled around painting pictures of different places, which were then made into woodblock prints. These became sort of like postcards and were even used for wrapping paper, so many were lost, but he did hundreds and hundreds of different views—and out of these about ten masterpieces."

"Effie, it sounds like you're back to being more interested in art than birds."

"Maybe so. I'm interested in everything. It makes it hard to concentrate on one thing. Especially with a baby."

"Can I talk to Corinne?"

"I'm putting her ear next to the phone."

"Hi, Corinne. It's your big brother. Hope you're . . . uh . . . feeling good and getting lots of milk and stuff. Don't forget me, okay?"

{26} Conclusion of T'ai Chi

I entered the apartment at 2:30 A.M. As usual, Mom had left a lamp lit in the living room with a snack on the coffee table in case I was hungry, but I was always too tired to be hungry. Everyone was asleep. We all had our own rooms, except Corinne was in with me. The other E's had their doors open so they could hear Corinne if she cried before I got home.

I stripped, put my waitress uniform in the hamper, washed haphazardly, and, dead on my feet, fell into bed. The next thing I knew, Ellie or Edna was putting Corinne in my arms for the 7 A.M. nursing, which I did while mostly still asleep. Then someone took her away to her high chair, which she had just begun using, so she could have her rice cereal and be sociable. Ellie was the first to go out the door. Her secretarial job at an import-export firm began at eight. Next to go was Edna, who worked as a receptionist at a detective agency like my namesake, Effie, had for Sam Spade in San Francisco. Before she left, she woke me up so I could do my T'ai Chi down in Washington Square before Mom left for work at her law firm.

It was so wonderful that, right outside our apartment in

North Beach, the Italian section of San Francisco, fast becoming Asianized, was Washington Square (quixotically honored by a statue of Ben Franklin) and in the square, every morning, about thirty people gathered to greet the day with T'ai Chi. We met in front of the cathedral of St. Peter and Paul with its beautiful twin spires. The builders of this Catholic church never dreamed the day would come when Chinese people would do ancient calisthenics before its portals. My people! I'd found my tribe.

I tumbled from bed, pulled on my sweats, stumbled down the three flights, and walked the one and a half blocks. Everyone was milling around, waiting to begin. I loved the milling part and the exotic high-pitched chatter. I loved how the milling stopped, silence descended, and everyone stood facing different ways, with just enough space between them, and then began.

We went through the form three times. The group energy was sublime. No matter that all kinds of different variations were being practiced, I had my little group of Cheng Man-ch'ing-ites over by the statue honoring San Francisco firemen.

Mom arrived with Corinne in her infant seat and set her on a nearby bench, where she could watch the hopping and pecking of a bunch of grackles. Mom chatted with some of the park loiterers then went on her way to work. My students showed up and I began to teach.

"Inhaling slowly, raise your hands to shoulder height. Mobilize your *chi* and extend your fingers . . ."

An hour later, back in the apartment, I had breakfast: caffè latte, cereal, and fruit. I felt happy and energized. I would have the day with Corinne until I went to the restaurant at six. We would have a two-hour nap in the afternoon, although probably I would read. It was my only time to read. In five years, when Corinne went to school, I'd catch up on my sleep. Sometime during the day, I'd try to bird-watch somewhere, but I was doing it less and less.

The main thing was: The family was together and we were

all getting by and it was fine to have our own rooms. We all contributed to household expenses except Mom, whom we were making save money to go to law school starting next fall. More and more folks were coming to my T'ai Chi class. They paid ten dollars a week and could come as often as they wanted. Soon I could cut back on my waitressing.

Both Gled and Martha sent me money sporadically, but I was investing their contributions for Corinne's college education. Sometimes Gled gave me the money in person, as he'd kept the job jet-chauffeuring the mysterious San Francisco philanthropist. Leading a bicoastal life, he often brought Danny out with him and Corinne and I got to be with him. Sometimes Gled came to see Corinne even if I wasn't home. He finally realized she was totally enchanting, maybe because her hair was getting curly, her eyes brown. I'd told him Martha said there had only been blue eyes in her family for centuries.

On my night off, if Gled was in town, he urged me to visit him at his apartment without Corinne or my mother or sisters, but so far I'd resisted. I simply tied myself to the leg of the dining room table and had Ellie or Edna bring me Scotch and food and books. I couldn't give Gled back to Lynn and Danny only to take him away first chance I got. They needed him. They were frail. I was tough as nails. I think he knew I loved him. I longed for him, but I was okay for now, sort of. Crane molts. Crane lies down with her legs sticking up in the air, her neck dragging on the ground.

Maybe I wasn't being noble so much as I was depriving myself to make up for the wrong I'd done Alan.

Had I wronged Alan?

During our final scene, I hadn't defended myself to him (never explain, never complain), but when he accused me of making love to another man on my honeymoon, I could have said it was only one time and then only because I'd fallen in the quarry, been hit on the head, and given brandy in front of a badly lit fire, so I was not answerable for my actions. I could have told him that, upon finding myself pregnant, I was definitely going to tell him about Gled had he not told me to abort Corinne.

No, I didn't wrong Alan. I was only riding the tiger.

So I wasn't punishing myself. I really was noble.

Ellie and Edna were great and they never tired of my telling them about the rustic rest room incident, feeling unconditionally horrified as only sisters can, not being critical or wondering where they went wrong or putting down a real large emotion as a paltry panic attack. The best way to remember things is to tell them to a willing audience. Even if the content changes in the telling, the story gets better and more true and more integrated into one's life.

Danny loves the story of how his dad came in the nick of time and slammed into the door again and again until it opened and he saved us from everything: the mountain lions, the dark, the cement, the being in a trap.

I tell Corinne, believing as I have from day one that she is a conscious person, but I modify the story a lot for her, not wanting to scare her. I can embroider as she gets older, but how much do you tell your daughter? How much has Mom ever told me? There are just so many places in raising a daughter, that, as a mother, you can go wrong.

While I was washing up all our breakfast dishes, the phone rang.

"Hello, darling?"

"Hi, Martha."

"We haven't talked in a while. How's Corinne?"

I waxed enthusiastic about Corinne for five minutes.

"And how are you, Effie?"

"I'm great."

"We're worried about your mind rotting."

"Who's we?"

"Janice. I'm in New York and we've just had breakfast together. We have a wonderful idea. We want you to write your bigamist's story."

"I'm not a writer."

"You wrote half a thesis!"

"You know what I mean. I'm not a real writer, not an artist. I'm not talented."

"Yes, you are, Effie. I snooped once and read your journal."

"How could you?"

"I studied Gregg shorthand as a teenager. I had a job on a newspaper and did interviews and used shorthand."

"I meant, how could you be so villainous . . . ?"

"It was enthralling. And, Effie, just think. You'd be able to work at home and could give up the waitressing. You'd be using your brain. We could get you an advance on a few chapters and an outline—although nothing like Alan's, you understand. You're not the same product. Although you are young and pretty. Are you pretty? Did you lose weight?"

"Please forget it, Martha."

"I'm afraid I can't."

"You mean, you'll write it if I don't."

"Heavens, I wouldn't know how to begin. Although, come to think of it, I'd probably begin on the morning you first left Alan, virtually running away from the bridal bed, leaving the rings on the bedside table. What do you think?"

"I think I couldn't plunder everyone's personal lives. It's not fair."

"But, Effie, writers don't think about *fair.*"

I laughed. "You write it. I'm doing what I want and my mind is fine. I'm taking everything I've learned about art and love and birds and family and I'm becoming a teacher."

"But where will you teach? Harvard?"

I laughed again. "No. Outdoors. In the park. Then, when winter comes, maybe at the Y."

"Oh! T'ai Chi. What a good idea!"

"I've only practiced for eight years, but I'm beginning to get it and I think I have something to impart. I'm happy."

"I'm so proud of you, Effie."

After I hung up, I stood relaxed, toes forward, arms down, open hands loosely hanging beside my thighs, legs straight, slightly bent at the knee, head high, backbone aligned, nose and navel in line. I was smiling. It was the stance for the Conclusion of T'ai Chi, which is also the stance for the Beginning of T'ai Chi.

Corinne Ryan's Lagoon House Yard List

Compiled by Peter Pyle
and Keith Hansen
Bolinas, California

Loon, Red-throated
Pacific
Common

Grebe, Pied-billed
Horned
Eared
Red-necked
Western
Clark's

Fulmar, Northern

Shearwater, Sooty
Black-vented

Storm Petrel, Ashy

Pelican, White
Brown

Cormorant, Double-crested
Brant's
Pelagic

Heron, Great Blue
Green-backed

Night Heron, Black-crowned

Egret, Snowy
Great
Cattle

Swan, Tundra

Goose, Greater White-fronted
Snow
Ross's
Canada
Brant

Duck, Wood

Teal, Green-winged
Cinnamon
Blue-winged

Shoveler, Northern

Mallard, Mallard

Pintail, Northern

Gadwall, Gadwell

Wigeon, American
Eurasian

Canvasback, Canvasback

Duck, Ring-necked

Scaup, Greater
Lesser

Duck, Harlequin

Oldsquaw, Oldsquaw

Scoter, White-winged
Surf
Black

Goldeneye, Common
Barrow's

Bufflehead, Bufflehead

Merganser, Common
Red-breasted

Duck, Ruddy

Vulture, Turkey

Osprey, Osprey

Kite, Black-shouldered

Eagle, Bald
Golden

Harrier, Northern

Hawk, Cooper's
Sharp-shinned
Red-shouldered
Red-tailed
Broad-winged
Ferruginous
Rough-legged

Kestrel, American

Merlin, Merlin

Falcon, Peregrine

Quail, California

Coot, American

Crane, Sandhill

Plover, Black-bellied
American Golden
Pacific Golden
Snowy
Semipalmated

Killdeer, Killdeer

Stilt, Black-necked

Avocet, American

Yellowlegs, Greater
Lesser

Willet, Willet

Tattler, Wandering

Sandpiper, Spotted

Whimbrel, Whimbrel

Curlew, Long-billed

Godwit, Marbled

Turnstone, Ruddy
Black

Surfbird, Surfbird

Knot, Red

Sanderling, Sanderling

Stint, Little

Sandpiper, Western
Semipalmated
Least
Baird's
Pectoral

Dunlin, Dunlin

Ruff, Ruff

Dowitcher, Long-billed
Short-billed

Snipe, Common

Phalarope, Red-necked
Red

Jaeger, Pomarine
Parasitic

Gull, Franklin's
Bonapart's
Heerman's
Mew
Ring-billed
California
Herring
Thayer's
Western
Glaucous-winged
Glaucous

Kittiwake, Black-legged

Tern, Caspian

Tern, Elegant
Common
Arctic
Forster's
Least
Black

Murre, Common

Guillemot, Pigeon

Murrelet, Marbled
Ancient

Auklet, Rhinoceros

Puffin, Tufted

Dove, Mourning

Pigeon, Band-tailed

Owl, Barn
Great Horned
Burrowing
Long-eared
Short-eared

Swift, Black
Vaux
White-throated

Hummingbird, Anna's
Black-chinned
Rufous
Allen's

Kingfisher, Belted

Woodpecker, Acorn
Nuttall's
Downy
Hairy

Flicker, Northern

Sapsucker, Red-breasted

Wood Pewee, Western

Flycatcher, Olive-sided
Willow
Least
Western

Phoebe, Black
Say's

Flycatcher, Ash-throated

Kingbird, Western

Lark, Horned

Martin, Purple

Swallow, Tree
Violet-green
Rough-winged
Bank
Cliff
Barn

Jay, Steller's
Scrub

Crow, American

Raven, Common

Chickadee, Chestnut-backed

Bushtit, Bushtit

Nuthatch, Red-breasted
Pygmy

Creeper, Brown

Wren, Bewick's
House
Winter

Kinglet, Golden-crowned
Ruby-crowned

Gnatcatcher, Blue-gray

Bluebird, Western

Thrush, Swainson's
Hermit
Varied

Robin, American

Wrentit, Wrentit

Mockingbird, Northern

Pipit, Water
Red-throated

Waxwing, Cedar

Shrike, Loggerhead

Vireo, Hutton's
Solitary
Warbling

Warbler, Orange-crowned
Nashville
Yellow
Chestnut-sided
Magnolia
Yellow-rumped
Black-throated Gray
Townsend's
Hermit
Black-throated Green
Blackburnian
Palm
Bay-breasted
Black and white

Redstart, American

Warbler, Mac Gillivray's
Wilson's

Yellowthroat, Common

Chat, Yellow-breasted

Tanager, Western
Summer

Grosbeak, Black-headed
Evening

Bunting, Lazull
Indigo

Towee, Rufous-sided
Brown

Sparrow, Chipping
Lark
Savannah
Fox
Song
Lincoln's

Sparrow, White-throated
Golden-crowned

Junco, Dark-eyed

Longspur, Lapland

Blackbird, Red-winged
Tricolored
Brewer's

Cowbird, Brown-headed

Oriole, Northern
Hooded

Finch, Purple
House

Crossbill, Red

Siskin, Pine

Goldfinch, Lesser
American